THE ENGLISH AU PAIR

Stella Lazenby flies to Spain to work as an au pair for Isabel and Ignacio Mendoza, looking after their sons Juan and Javier. The parents are charming, the boys delightful — and then there's the handsome Stefano, who becomes more than a friend . . . But all is not as perfect as it seems. Housekeeper Maria resents Stella's presence, and Isabel worries that her husband is hiding secrets. Then Stefano is accused of stealing from Ignacio's company, and Stella doesn't know what to believe . . .

CHRISSIE LOVEDAY

---◆---

THE
ENGLISH
AU PAIR

Complete and Unabridged

LINFORD
Leicester

First published in Great Britain in 2019

First Linford Edition
published 2020

A catalogue record for this book is available
from the British Library.

ISBN 978–1–4448–4574–7

Mixed Reception

The plane flew lower as it prepared to land. Stella peered out of the window at the mass of high-rise apartment buildings dotting the horizon. She could catch glimpses of the sea in the distance — deepest blue and sparkling in the sunshine. Then she could see rows of massive buildings and wondered who on earth could fill them all.

She was arriving in Alicante. She had a thrill of excitement and wondered for the umpteenth time what the family would be like.

This was Stella's first trip to Spain. Her mother had died a few weeks ago, and once she had cleared away all the borrowed aids and returned them to the health service, the flat seemed very empty, as did her whole future.

She was almost twenty-five and had looked after her mother for the past 10 years. Her frail condition and deteriorating health had seemed such a burden to the girl until her mother had finally succumbed.

Now, Stella had begun her new life. She had answered an advertisement for an au pair with a family living in southern Spain, through an agency, who had seemed impressed with her abilities and recommended her to the family.

As far as she knew, she would be responsible for two little boys who were at private school during the term time. It sounded a perfect job, not too demanding, and she had always been fond of children.

Her time spent looking after her mother had certainly equipped her for a role as carer for any age group.

The plane bumped down and she felt a sudden panic, not entirely at the motion but the thought of meeting new people and starting a completely new job. Suppose they didn't like her or she didn't like them? It was a long way from home — not that she exactly had a home to go back to, if it didn't work out.

Stella picked up her hand luggage and was ready to disembark. She went through customs and went to collect her large bag. She had left a lot of her things distributed around various friends who had space to store them and she planned to collect them when she was next in the UK. When would that be, she wondered.

Hesitantly, Stella walked through into the meeting area after clearing customs. She stared round to see who would be waiting for her. There seemed to be lots of people who stepped forward and greeted friends and relations as well as holiday reps collecting their groups.

She saw someone with a piece of card with her name on it and stepped forward expectantly. He was much younger than she was expecting.

'Hello. I'm Stella Lazenby,' she said, smiling at the man. He didn't look

3

much older than her. If he was the parent of two boys, he must have married very young, she was thinking.

'Hi, there. I'm Stefano. I work for Mr Mendoza.'

'Oh, I thought you were Mr Mendoza, only perhaps a bit too young.'

He laughed, and Stella couldn't help thinking how handsome he was.

'You will see, I don't look anything like him. He has grey hair for a start.'

'My mistake. I must say, you speak excellent English.'

'My mother is English. My father is Spanish. He left us years ago. We speak English most of the time at home. You'll find the Mendozas all speak English, too, most of the time. Mrs Mendoza is also English. Now, let's get back to the car. I'll carry your bag.'

'It's all right, thanks. It's on wheels so it will pull along.'

'Please, allow me.'

Stella gave in gracefully and found herself almost running to keep up with him. They reached the car and she gave a silent gasp. It was huge and looked very luxurious.

Stefano opened the boot and stowed her case. He asked if she wanted to put in her hand baggage but she declined, saying she would keep it with her.

'You want to travel in the back or the front?' Stefano asked.

'I'd prefer the front so we can talk more easily.'

He nodded and opened the door for her. She felt like a privileged lady as she settled down into the luxurious comfort.

'This is very nice. Thank you.'

'It's Mr Mendoza's own car. He had a meeting this afternoon so he asked me to fetch you.'

'Are you his . . . well, his chauffeur?'

'Goodness me, no! I'm in charge of computer services for the company. He usually drives himself but asked me to come to the airport.

'I must say, I do enjoy driving this car. Bit different from mine. I've got an ancient Ford. Still, it gets me around.

I'll have to take you out in it one day. You may even notice the slight difference between the two cars.

'You know the sort of thing, a crash when the gear changes happen and brakes that screech a bit.'

'You make it sound irresistible. I shall look forward to it. How far is it from the airport?'

'About two hours. This isn't actually the closest airport to their home, but Mr Mendoza was looking at where was most convenient for you to get on the plane.'

'That was kind of him.'

They travelled along motorways until he suddenly turned off. It was strange to Stella to be driving on the wrong side of the road and suddenly to swoop along a break on her right. She was so pleased she wasn't in charge of the vehicle or expected to drive so large a machine, especially a left hand drive.

They chatted freely and Stella felt much more at ease. At last, Stefano pulled into a long drive and stopped outside a large house.

'Wow, this looks nice. Magnificent, in fact.' Stella suddenly felt very nervous. She had burned her boats by leaving the rented flat and here she was a stranger in a strange land. It was only April but already she felt very warm. 'I suppose there's nothing else for it but to get out and meet people,' she muttered.

'Sorry? What did you say?' Stefano asked.

'Nothing important.' She got out of the car and went round to collect her bag.

'It's OK. I'll get it,' he offered. She stood nervously waiting as he opened the boot and lifted out her luggage. Stefano rang the doorbell and they stood together waiting. A dark-haired woman opened it.

'Maria, this is Stella. She's here to look after the boys. Stella, this is Maria, the housekeeper.'

'Pleased to meet you,' Stella said,

holding out her hand. It was ignored.

'You'd better come in. The Señora say she be coming soon. Thank you, Stefano. You'll need to get back to the office.'

Stefano put her case down and handed over the other bag.

'Thank you very much for fetching me. I hope to see you again soon.'

'My pleasure. I hope to see you, too. Bye, then.'

'Bye.' Stella watched him go back to the car and drive away. 'Now, where would you like me to go?' she asked the housekeeper.

'Back to where you come from,' Maria said with a snarl.

'I'm sorry? What do you mean?'

'Nothing. You can go upstairs. Your room is ready for you.'

'And which room is mine?'

'Top of stairs. First right.' Obviously the woman resented her arrival for some reason. Stella picked up her suitcase and went up the broad staircase. She saw a long corridor with several doors and quickly found her room.

It was a beautiful room with a large bed and an en suite to one side. There were net curtains and also electric blinds which came down on the outside of the building.

Stella pushed open the doors and discovered a balcony with a small table and two chairs. It overlooked a lovely but quite small garden, filled with exotic plants and tall palm trees.

Wow, she was thinking. This was such a beautiful place to be. She went back inside and opened the built-in wardrobe. It was massive. Her few clothes were going to look lost in there. Shelves down one side provided a place for her to leave smaller items.

Feeling much happier, she opened her case and took out her dresses and trousers and hung them up. So, if the housekeeper didn't like her, then she would just have to avoid her as much as possible.

Stella glanced at her watch. It was

3.30. It must be nearly time for the boys to be home from school. She went down the stairs and looked around for someone to ask.

The lounge was at the bottom of the stairs to one side. It had views over the sea and was large enough to house several sofas and coffee tables. The charming room didn't look English in any way.

Stella turned away and went through a door at the side. This led into a dining-room. Again, it was beautifully appointed with a long dining table and several chairs down each side. Obviously this was a couple who entertained regularly.

She could imagine a group of people dressed smartly, sitting round eating a delicious meal. A door on the other side led into the kitchen. This was Maria's territory and she entered with a degree of caution after the reception she had met when she arrived.

'What you want?' the housekeeper demanded.

'I was just looking around and saw this door. Sorry if I'm intruding. I was wondering when the boys come home. And anyone else, come to that.'

'Dunno. You have wait and see. Now, if you not mind . . . ' she said in a thick accent.

'Sorry,' Stella said again. 'I'll go and wait in my room.' She went back upstairs and took out her tablet. She clicked to see if she had any e-mails. Nothing that needed replies. She pulled up a card game and played with that for a few minutes. This wasn't at all what she had been expecting.

As far as she knew, Mrs Mendoza didn't work so where was she this afternoon? She switched off her tablet and went downstairs again.

Stella went out in the garden. It was quite a small plot, as most of the house took up the space with its terraces and patios. She wasn't used to the Spanish lifestyle of sitting on terraces instead of on lawns.

She heard a commotion going on

11

inside the house and went back inside. The boys had arrived home from school, brought there by their mother. Stella was suddenly shocked to see Mrs Mendoza in a wheelchair.

'Hello. You must be Stella. I'm so sorry I wasn't here to greet you. I hope Maria made you feel at home.'

'How do you do. It's lovely to meet you. And you two must be Javier and Juan? Which is which?' To her surprise they stood side by side and bowed as they spoke.

'I am Juan,' the older one said.

'I am Javier,' the little one said as he bowed.

'My name is Stella and I'm very pleased to meet you. I hope we shall all be friends.' She avoided the question about Maria making her feel at home. The woman had behaved in quite the opposite way. Stella didn't understand why but it was not something she was going to make a fuss about.

'OK, boys, time for homework. Go into the study and settle down.'

'Can't we have a drink and some cookies first?' Juan asked.

'Please, please, please,' Javier said.

'OK. Go and ask Maria. Only one cookie each though,' their mother instructed. The two of them went off through the door Stella considered the forbidden door. 'They always try it on when they come home. I hope you were offered a drink, and perhaps something to eat.'

'Well, no. Maria was busy and I didn't like to ask for anything.'

'Goodness me. What must you think of our hospitality? I'll ring for her to bring something right away.' Mrs Mendoza moved easily to one side of the room and pressed a bell. Maria arrived a few moments later looking slightly annoyed.

'Madame,' she said.

'You didn't offer our visitor anything when she arrived.'

'She didn't ask for anything.'

'I would have expected you to offer. Perhaps you could bring some tea and perhaps a sandwich and some cake or something.'

'If you say so, madame.' She swung round and left the room looking very grumpy.

'Goodness me. I don't know what's wrong with the woman. She's never behaved like this before.'

'Perhaps she resents me coming into her territory and perhaps muscling in on her duties.'

'Hmm. I don't know about that. She's in a bad mood for some reason. She is a good cook and usually a reliable housekeeper. Obviously, I am not able to do much myself.'

Stella was on the brink of asking her what had happened to put her in a wheelchair but decided against it. She would undoubtedly find out at some point and didn't want to risk causing any unpleasantness.

'You must be wondering why I am in this wheelchair,' Mrs Mendoza said, almost as if she had read Stella's mind. The girl nodded.

'I was in an accident, a car accident, and I broke my back. I can't really walk at all and am reliant on help in the house and now, your help with the boys. We do have someone who comes to clean so you'd never have to do anything like that.'

'I'm so sorry to hear that. About your accident, I mean. Perhaps it might improve one day? Oh, and I wouldn't mind helping out in the house a little.'

'Well, thank you. I would like you to drive the boys to school each morning and collect them afterwards. You can use the small car we keep for such things.'

'I'm glad I wouldn't have to drive your husband's car. It's enormous.'

'I don't like driving it, either. I have my own car, too, which is specially adapted for my needs. I only go out in the big car when we're going out for the evening.'

The two of them chatted easily for several minutes until the door opened and the two boys came through, one carrying a plate of sandwiches and the other with several biscuits on another plate. Maria arrived with a teapot and two cups and saucers. She put it down and left the room.

'Goodness me, she is in a bad mood,' Mrs Mendoza said. 'Whatever's brought that on?'

'She doesn't like having another English person in the house,' Javier announced. Stella looked embarrassed for a moment.

'What makes you say that?' his mother asked.

'She more or less said so.'

'What exactly did she say?' The two boys exchanged a glance but neither of them replied. 'Come on. I want to know.'

'She spoke in Spanish and you said we must only speak English in front of Stella.' Juan spoke clearly with a sweet smile on his face. Stella was immediately hooked and knew she was going to defend him whatever he said and whenever he spoke.

16

'On this occasion you may speak in Spanish,' their mother told them.

They babbled something in Spanish that Stella couldn't understand. She made a resolution to learn some Spanish as soon as possible.

'I see . . . I'll have a word or two with her later. Now, perhaps you could pass the sandwiches to Stella and I'll pour the tea.'

Juan held out the plate towards her and she took one. She bit into it and practically choked. It was thick with mayo and she absolutely hated the stuff. She struggled through it and felt sick by the time she had finished it. Washed down with tea, she felt a bit better but refused any more.

'Is there something wrong?' Mrs Mendoza asked.

'I'm not a great fan of mayo, that's all.'

'Oh, poor you. I'll tell Maria and hopefully that will be the end of it.'

'Wouldn't bank on it,' Javier remarked quietly. His mother ignored him.

17

'Go on, then. One more biscuit each and then you must go and make a start on homework.' Gleefully the boys each pounced on a biscuit and disappeared from the room.

'They are good boys,' Stella observed. 'I'm going to enjoy being with them. And I'd like to try to learn some Spanish. I did French at school.'

'If you already have knowledge of another language, I'm sure it won't be too difficult for you. I think the boys would love to help you, too. It would be good for them.

'Now, go on, off to do your homework, you two.' The door opened and two faces smiled round it. 'Go on. To your rooms, rather than the study.'

'How did you know they were still there?' Stella asked, laughing.

'Instinct. One learns quickly. Case of needs must. We have a lift so I can get upstairs easily. Our room is on this level but I need to go and look at the boys' rooms occasionally. I manage very well.'

Stella couldn't help but admire this

woman. She couldn't be very old and it must have come as a terrible shock to her, making such a difference to their lifestyle.

The family were obviously pretty well off and so money wasn't a problem. They had bought in help to keep the house going, hence her own new role.

'It must have taken a lot of getting used to. The accident, I mean. A big change in your lives.'

'Oh, it certainly was. My husband was also injured but he recovered well. It's certainly taken a long time. The boys were only babies so we had to make arrangements for them. I suppose we were lucky to have plenty of money.'

'Thank you for telling me. It must have been so hard for you but you've overcome it all now. Do you think it will ever be possible for you to walk again?' Stella paused and bit her tongue. How on earth could she have been so insensitive?

'I'm sorry ... I wasn't thinking. Please forgive me.'

19

'Not at all. It's a perfectly natural thing to ask. I'm afraid not. I don't think it's possible for me to be able to walk properly again but Ignacio is very understanding and helps me so much.

'Now, I must go and change and perhaps you could go and see how the boys are getting on.'

Stella smiled and went upstairs to find the boys' rooms.

'How's it going?' she asked Juan when she had knocked at his door.

'OK. Do you know what seven times twelve is?'

'I do. Don't you?'

'I can't remember.'

'Try saying your seven times table till you get there.'

'Be much quicker if you told me,' the little boy said, with a wicked twinkle in his eye.

'What are seven times eleven?'

'Easy peasy. Seventy-seven.'

'And so what is another seven added to that?' He counted on his fingers and smiled and said eighty-four. 'OK, so now you know what seven times twelve is.'

'I didn't know you could add the number to get the multiplication sort of stuff. I thought they were quite separate. Good. I've learned something. *Gracias*.'

'*Gracias*.'

'No, you should say *de nada*.'

'What does that mean?'

' It's nothing — you're welcome. Most polite people and waiters in restaurants say it all the time.'

'OK. My first lesson in Spanish. I'm going to see Javier now.'

'He'll be playing with his cars, you just wait and see. He always does that.'

'Doesn't he have homework?'

'Not really. Usually he has to draw a picture or something really easy like that.'

'I suppose he still is only a little boy.'

'I had homework when I was only a little boy.'

Stella laughed.

'I'll leave you to it.'

Happy Families

Stella went to the next room along the corridor where Javier gave a guilty jump as she knocked and opened the door.

'Hello,' she said, smiling.

'Hi. I was just starting my homework. It's English. I'm good at English.'

'I'm sure you are. Tell me what you have to do this evening.'

Javier went into a long explanation of answering questions and what he was going to put. She listened and made some suggestions. At last, she left him to it and went downstairs again.

Stella was keen to talk some more to Mrs Mendoza and find out exactly what her responsibilities were going to be. She felt a bit strange at the moment, not knowing what was expected of her. She didn't want to do the boys' homework for them.

Of course she was willing to help, but

there was a line to be drawn. At the moment it looked as if she was going to spend a lot of time on her own and this couldn't really be justified. In the lounge, Mrs Mendoza was reading the paper.

'I'm sorry to disturb you, Mrs Mendoza, but I need to talk to you. I need to know exactly what is expected of me.'

'Of course you do. I think you should call me Isabel. I can't be doing with all this formality.'

'Thank you. Isabel it is then.'

'And my husband is Ignacio. He won't think of telling you what you should call him so I'm telling you now.'

'If that's all right. Thank you. I haven't met him yet, of course.'

'Oh, but I thought he was collecting you from the airport.'

'Someone called Stefano collected me. He said your husband had a meeting and so he lent him his car and sent him instead.'

'That's typical. So, you've met our

handsome Stefano? How did you get on?'

'Very well. He seemed very friendly and nice. I gather he does something with computers.'

'He certainly does. He's indispensable to the company. Very talented chap. I'm surprised he could be spared for the afternoon. He's usually totally bogged down with things that need doing.'

They chatted about various topics for a while. Stella was soon happy enough with what was expected of her. She would spend the days pretty much on her own, sometimes with Isabel, if she was needed to help her with shopping. She would take the boys to school and fetch them home again.

During the holidays, she would be expected to take them out and generally entertain them. There was an indoor pool in the basement apparently and they both needed to make sure they could swim safely.

The English girl was delighted at this

24

prospect as she had always enjoyed swimming and had even been on her school team at one point.

'That's lovely, dear. I'm sure you'll be a great hit with both of them.'

'I wasn't sure how much I should help them with their homework,' Stella said.

'Now there's a problem. They will always ask you to help them, even when they know full well what the answers are. Typical little boys. Javier is the worst. His attention span is somewhat limited.'

'I did notice he was playing with toy cars instead of doing his writing. He did settle down to his homework after I spoke to him.'

'I think that's the best way to deal with him. If you don't mind helping them a bit, that would be great. Perhaps you won't be able to help them a great deal, especially with the Spanish elements. But thank you.

'Tomorrow, I'll go with you to school so you know where it is and then perhaps we can do a bit of shopping and maybe have some lunch.'

'That sounds wonderful. Thank you. What happens with meals in the evenings?'

'The boys usually have dinner with us around seven. If we are entertaining, they eat earlier and then go off to bed. This doesn't happen more than once a week.

'We would like you to join us when this happens. You can put the boys to bed earlier and then change and come to meet some of our friends.'

'That's very good of you. Don't forget my Spanish is virtually non-existent. I'd be happy to eat with the boys and stay in my room.'

'Let's see how it goes. Now then, I need a short rest before Ignacio gets home. He promised he'd be early tonight so he could spend time getting to know you. Will you be all right for a while?'

'Of course.'

Stella watched as Isabel wheeled

herself professionally through the door and disappeared into her room. What a lovely lady she seemed to be. There was such a contrast between her and Maria, she was thinking somewhat uncharitably.

The housekeeper/cook must have a problem today or at least Stella hoped it was just today. If she was going to be as difficult all the time, life was not going to be so good. The woman worked in a home where English was spoken most of the time so surely she couldn't be prejudiced against her for that reason?

She sat down and idly glanced at the paper Isabel had been reading. There wasn't much that interested her as she didn't know the area at all or any of the people. She flicked through it and came to a piece written by a Mr Ignacio Mendoza.

She couldn't really understand what it was about, despite the fact it was written in English. It was obviously written by the Mr Mendoza who lived here. At least she would have something to ask him about. Perhaps he might explain something about his business so at least she could understand his article.

Maria came into the room.

'What you do here?' she demanded.

'Just reading the local newspaper.'

'Why you not with boys?'

'They're doing their homework. I did go to help them but now they are finishing it.'

'My niece would no leave them. She always stay with them. Not you, though. You lazy girl.'

'I'm sorry? Whatever do you mean?'

'You lazy girl. Leave boys on their own. You get her job. Not right.'

'I see. I'm sorry your niece didn't get the job but Mr and Mrs Mendoza wanted an English au pair for their boys.'

'My niece, she speak good English. She much better than you. She never leave boys on their own. She not lazy. Now, you go see them. I need to set table for dinner.'

For a moment, Stella thought of ignoring the housekeeper and staying exactly where she was but she decided to leave the unpleasant woman to her own devices. She went upstairs to Javier's room and knocked at the door and opened it.

'How are you getting on?' she asked.

'I'm very bored. I feel much too tired to do any more homework.'

'Let me see what you've done so far,' Stella asked him.

'I've done tons. All my English and I've looked at some sums. I don't have to do them till tomorrow.'

'Very good. Show me your answers in the English homework.' He held out his page for her to look at. It was very untidy but his answers all seemed correct. 'You need to make your writing much clearer but well done.'

'Will you show me how to write more clearly?' he asked. His little face was so intense, she wanted to give him a big hug. 'I'm not very good at writing.'

'Of course I will.' Stella needed to dig

deep in her memory for the far off lessons she had done in the past when she was at primary school. She remembered her teacher giving them sheets of letters they were supposed to copy.

'Do you know the English alphabet?' Stella asked. 'Let's do it together.'

Together they recited the whole alphabet and the little boy clapped his hands in delight.

'I always forget some of the letters but with you there, it was much better.'

'I'm glad. We can try it again tomorrow if you like.'

'Yes, please. Then I'll be able to say it all by myself.'

They chatted for a while longer and then he asked if he could go downstairs now. Evidently they usually did when they had finished their homework. Stella thought it was a bit much for them to have so much to do on their own, at such a young age.

Still, who was she to argue about a foreign system? It was, after all, a private school and possibly they had different rules.

'I'll see how Juan is getting on and then we'll go down together if that's what you usually do.' She wondered what Maria would say to that idea, having been told in no uncertain terms to get herself out of the woman's way. She went over to Juan. He was staring out of his window looking totally bored.

'How are you getting on?' she asked.

'I'm not. This stupid map I'm supposed to draw doesn't make any sense. I mean to say, how do I know what fruit we grow in Spain? I'm supposed to colour in various different areas where they grow things.'

'What did your teacher tell you about this?'

'Dunno.'

'She or he must have said something about it before giving you this as homework.'

'It's a she. Senora Gonzales. She hates me and never tells me what I should do. She wants me to sort it out for myself and I never know what I'm supposed to do.'

'I'm sure she doesn't dislike you.'

'Oh, yes, she does. Her husband got sacked from Dad's company and she takes it out on me. It's not fair.'

'Well, perhaps she's sad because her husband lost his job. I'm sure she doesn't deliberately stop you from knowing what your homework is.'

'Oh, but she does.'

'Let's think, then. What fruit do you know is grown in Spain?'

'I don't know,' he replied sullenly.

'What fruit do you like?'

'Peaches and apricots.'

'Are they grown in Spain?'

'I suppose so. Apples.'

'I think apples are grown everywhere, just about.'

'Oranges. Strawberries. Tomatoes — they grow loads of them.'

'So, there's a good start for you. Let me see your map.'

Juan showed her the outline he had been given and very soon, they found areas he could colour in to represent different fruits.

'Thank you, miss. That was very helpful of you.'

'I thought you were going to call me Stella.' She laughed.

'I am. You seemed like a teacher, though.'

'I'm not a teacher. Just an au pair.'

'I like au pairs if they're like you. Can we go down now?'

'Of course. What shall we do?'

'We can show you our playroom. It's pretty cool. Do you like Minecraft?'

'Well, not really. I take it you have a computer with it all on.'

'We do. We have to share it, though. It's an old one of Dad's so if we break it, it doesn't really matter.'

The two boys chatted all the way downstairs, each of them vying to dominate the chatter. They led the way into the playroom. It was a lovely room with large wide windows overlooking the garden.

There were built-in cupboards along

one side and a work bench down the other side with a variety of Lego models in various stages of construction. A large computer was set up at one end of the bench and there was an electric piano and even a snooker table in the middle of the room.

'My goodness. You have everything you could want in here. How lovely.' Stella was amazed at so many things the boys had, especially when they opened the cupboards and she saw rows of games, books and other toys.

'Do you want to see our Minecraft?' Juan asked.

'Well, yes, please.' She'd heard of it and knew it was the current obsession with many youngsters but had little or no idea of what it actually was.

As she watched, she realised Juan was almost an expert in use of the computer. She was several million miles behind his expertise. He pulled up an entire village with houses, hotels and things she could scarcely recognise.

'Goodness me. You are so clever,' she said admiringly. 'You leave me behind well and truly.' The little boy blushed with pleasure at her words.

'Dad wanted us to be used to using computers. He thinks the future will lie in everyone being able to use them properly. I want to go into business like my dad.'

Stella was surprised at his ambition but it was possibly likely that he admired his father and his business sense.

'I hope you do,' was her best answer.

There was a slight noise and she half rose to open the door. Isabel came into the room, waving her hand in dismissal as there was a mechanical device to open the door.

'How are you all getting along?' she asked.

'Very good,' both boys chorused together.

'She knows . . . I mean Stella knows all about the fruit we eat here,' Juan told his mother excitedly.

'And about alphabets. We can do it together and always get it right,' Javier announced. 'Shall we do it now?'

'If you like.' His mother laughed. He went to stand by Stella and they began, with the au pair beginning letters when he forgot. 'Very well done, darling. I hope you thanked Stella for helping you.'

'Oh yes, they both did.'

'Good. Well, Daddy's on his way home so we shall soon be having dinner. You'd better go and wash your hands ready.'

Stella felt slightly nervous about meeting this evidently successful businessman. She didn't really know what she should call him for a start but perhaps he would make it clear when they met. A new sound came through the house. It was the garage door opening and closing again.

'There's Ignacio.' They went out of the playroom to wait in the main room. There was the sound of voices, male voices talking together.

36

'He must have brought someone home with him,' Isabel said. 'Oh dear. I hope Maria doesn't get cross with us all. Hello darling,' she called out as they came into the room.

The guest was Stefano. Stella was delighted to see him again and so soon.

'I thought we should invite Stefano to dine with us. He was instrumental in bringing this lovely lady to our home. Hello, Stella, I am Ignacio. I hope you will be happy here with us. Now where are those two rascals?' He left the room and began to search the house.

'Are they in the kitchen doing the cooking? Or are they in the cloakroom?'

There was the sound of a loud giggle and he flung open the door of the cloakroom.

'Found them. Have they been good boys, Mummy? Done their homework?'

Two little faces were grinning in delight at being discovered. Their father picked them up and tucked them under his arms.

'So, Stella, have they been good?'

'They certainly have. Homework all done and ready for tomorrow.'

'That is excellent. Perhaps they may have a tiny smidge of jam to go with their dry bread tonight. What do you think, Mummy?'

'Definitely. Only a tiny bit, though.' The boys were wriggling till they could escape their father's restraint and still laughing. Stefano was watching, smiling at all the family activity. He came to stand beside Stella.

'So, how are you getting on? Everything going well?'

'I think so. Maria is my only problem. Evidently her niece wanted the job and she is determined I should go home and leave the job for this girl.'

'The girl would never do. She hardly speaks any English. She's a rather coarse local girl, always out to catch the boys.'

Before Stella could respond, Ignacio came over to them.

'What would you like to drink?' he asked the two of them. 'How about a glass of Cava? We have some good Cava.'

'That sounds wonderful, thank you.' Stella looked round at the handsome family. Isabel was very pretty, a dark blonde with clear blue eyes.

Ignacio was still relatively young but prematurely grey-haired. He had obviously been dark-haired and had brown eyes, so typical of Spain. He was very good-looking and both boys favoured him. They also had dark hair and brown eyes and ready grins.

As for Stefano, he still attracted her very much. She felt she was going to be happy here, if only Maria could begin to cope with her role.

'Here we are, Stella,' Ignacio said, handing her a crystal glass. He handed one to his wife and Stefano and raised his glass. 'Let us drink a toast of welcome to Stella. We hope you will be happy during your stay in our house.' They all chorused cheers, including the two boys who drank their toast in lemonade.

'Thank you all very much. I'm sure it will all work out well and I hope I can be of service to you.'

'Hey, but that sounds rather formal. We hope you will become as one of the family. A young relation of my beautiful wife, perhaps.'

'I'd be honoured to be thought of in that way,' Stella mumbled shyly.

'And Stefano here, he is like an older brother to my boys. I hope you two will become great friends.'

Ignacio was nothing if not direct, she was thinking. Goodness me, she had scarcely been in the house for an afternoon before he was looking at her being related to his wife and possibly getting much closer to his employee.

Fortunately, at this point, Maria came and announced that dinner was ready. Stella followed them to the table. She felt a bit nervous, not knowing what food would be served and praying there was no more mayo.

The meal began with *jamon*, the delicious preserved Spanish ham cut in very thin slices. They ate this with slices of olive bread. Ignacio pressed her to eat more and more of it but she drew back, noticing there was a collection of cutlery which indicated at least two or more courses.

Next came a chicken dish with an array of vegetables and finally a cheese board and more bread to eat with it. There was also a large bunch of delicious looking grapes. Two different bottles of wine had been served and removed when everyone had a glass.

Then it was coffee and this was served with Limoncello liqueur to finish the meal.

Stella felt she might never eat again but she had really enjoyed everything.

'Bedtime now, boys,' Isabel said. They both leapt up from the table and murmured their goodnights to every-one.

'I'll come and read you a story in five minutes,' Ignacio told them. 'Five minutes is all the time you have to brush your teeth and get ready for bed.'

The two boys scuttled off laughing, knowing their father really meant what he said. He smiled at the rest of the party. 'They are not bad kids, are they?'

'You spoil them, Ignacio.'

'Spoil them? Nonsense. I'm the one person in this whole household who gets them moving. Two minutes to go.'

'Shall we go for a walk in the garden?' Stefano asked. 'Assuming you don't mind, Isabel?'

'Of course not. It's a gorgeous evening. You go and enjoy it. You might need a jacket or something. It can be chilly when the sun has gone.' Isabel was being thoughtful again. Stella realised what a very nice person she was and knew she was going to be happy in this house.

Forging Friendships

It wasn't a large garden but it had a series of paths which twisted round the house and between bushes. At the bottom of the garden, there was a platform which overlooked the sea. There were a couple of seats along this stretch and Stefano suggested they sit for a while.

The sea was almost invisible in the darkness but there were lots of boats anchored, with lights that shone their reflections into the calm sea. There were lights twinkling a short way along to one side, where the majority of beach bars and restaurants were situated.

'It gets incredibly busy along here in the summer. This is a good time to start your new life in Spain. You have time to get used to where you need to go and choose some of the quicker roads.

'For instance, taking the boys to their

school. There are possibly three differ-ent ways you can go. In the summer, you need to avoid what looks like the most direct route and take some of the back roads. I'm sure you'll soon get used to it all.'

'I'm a bit concerned about the heat. I need to watch out for sunburn.'

'You have a lovely English rose complexion which I always like but then, so do many Spaniards. You will need to be careful. These dark Spanish types, you know.'

'What — like you?'

'Oh, but I am very English. Take no notice of my dark hair and brown eyes.'

Stella smiled.

'But you are very good-looking.' Then she blushed at her own forward-ness.

'Well, thank you, ma'am. I'm glad you think so. You look pretty when you blush.'

'I hate it. Makes me feel sort of embarrassed. Childish, even.'

'You shouldn't. It shows you as a

sensitive person who cares about people.'

'You sound very wise. All the same, I hate my blushing. Nothing I can do about it. I say something and then feel my face getting hot. Will I ever get over it?'

'I'm told that older women don't seem to blush. So maybe once you reach seventy or something, you'll stop naturally.'

'Seventy? I doubt I'll ever make it to that age.'

'Why ever not?'

'My mum died recently and she was only in her fifties.' She suddenly felt tears filling her eyes at the thought of her mum. Her last years at school had been marred by looking after her and then she had only taken part-time jobs so she could be at home with Mum. This was a complete change to her life.

She was aware of her companion's arm slipping round her shoulders and he gave her a sympathetic squeeze.

Stella felt tears burning at the back of her eyes.

'You've had it tough. I'm glad you made the break and came here. I hope we shall be good friends and please, any time you need someone to talk to, call me.'

'That's kind of you. Thank you. I hope we shall be friends, too.' She was glad it was dark and he couldn't see her latest blushes and hoped he wasn't aware of her sudden, unexpected tears.

'Come on then. We'd better go inside before they send out a search party. Feel OK now?'

'I think so. I really think I shall be very happy here. The Mendozas do seem to be very kind.'

'They are wonderful. As long as you do what is expected of you and don't try to shirk your duties, they will respect you and treat you as one of the family.' They reached the door they had come out of and he pushed it open. 'In you go. I think Ignacio will have finished putting the boys to bed.'

Isabel was sitting in a chair looking at the paper.

'Come and sit down. Enjoy your walk?'

'Yes, thank you. It's a lovely garden,'

'Not very large but we've tried to make it seem larger with all the pathways.'

'I think you succeeded in that,' Stefano said quickly.

'Pity I can't really use it any more.' Isabel sighed. 'Still, I can sit out on the terraces and enjoy looking at it. I like to watch the boys when they play outside. I can tell them not to go anywhere they might hurt themselves.'

She had a wicked grin as she spoke and Stella realised she was completely at ease with her limitations. Isabel was a brave lady, she realised.

'Ah, so you're back,' Ignacio said, as he burst into the room like a whirlwind. 'What about drinks? What can I get for you all? More Cava? A liqueur, perhaps? Or brandy?'

'Goodness me, no, thank you.' Stella

laughed. 'I've already drunk far more than usual.'

'Stefano, then? What can I get for you?'

'I'd love a brandy but I still have to drive home so not for me, thank you.'

'Why not stay the night? Then it won't matter how much you have to drink.'

'I need to get back. My mother would never forgive me if I stayed away unexpectedly.'

'That is good. Always respect your mother. And Stella, how did your mother feel about you coming away?'

'My mother . . . ' She paused, trying to control her voice. 'My mother died recently. That was why . . . how I was able to come away.'

'Oh, my dear, I'm so sorry,' Isabel said. 'How very sad for you. Do you have a sister or brother?'

'No, no-one. My mum was very ill and I looked after her for a long time. It was a blessing in many ways as she was no longer in pain.'

'All the same, it must have been a terrible shock to you. You are very brave. We shall do all we can to make you feel welcome and at home, won't we, Ignacio?'

'Of course. And perhaps we should tell the boys to be sensitive to your emotions.'

'Oh no, please don't. I shall cope and probably feel better if they don't know about my past.'

They all nodded their agreement and the conversation continued about the area they lived in and places she could visit. Stella found herself yawning and realised it was almost 11 o'clock. She had been up early to catch her flight and now it was all catching up with her.

'I'm sorry but I think I need to go to bed soon,' she murmured. 'I suddenly feel very tired.'

'We've been keeping you up chatting for far too long. I hope you sleep well and we shall see you in the morning.' Isabel was very concerned that she was at fault.

'Oh no, I've really enjoyed my evening. It's wonderful that you've been so welcoming. I'm really going to enjoy being here with you all. Goodnight. Oh, what time in the morning?'

'The boys have to be at school for eight-thirty. That means leaving by eight at the latest. But please don't worry . . . I will take them tomorrow.' Ignacio was smiling as he spoke. 'Give you a chance for a lie in.'

'But I ought to know where to take them.'

'Isabel will show you later on when you collect them. Now, off you go and get some sleep.'

'OK, thank you. Goodnight, everyone.'

They all exchanged good wishes and she set off up the stairs. Despite feeling exhausted, sleep took a while to come and she lay there thinking of her day. It had been quite an adventure, starting in Cornwall and ending in Spain. Already she loved her two charges and the rest of the family all seemed very nice, too.

As for Stefano . . . well, that was quite another story. He must have the choice of dozens of girls here in Spain, so it was no use fixating on him. All the same . . .

* * *

Stella slept until well after the boys had gone to school. She awoke with a shock, dressed rapidly and almost ran downstairs.

'I'm so sorry. I took ages to fall asleep and then must have slept through my alarm.'

Isabel was still sitting at the breakfast table with a coffee.

'Ignacio took them to school. Don't worry about it. Come and have some breakfast. What would you like? We tend to have just toast and the boys have cereal, too.'

'Toast would be lovely. Shall I go and make some?'

'Maria will bring it.' She pressed a small bell at the side of the table and

Maria came into the room.

'Stella would like some toast and we'd both like some fresh coffee, please.' Maria nodded and glared at the girl. Obviously she hadn't yet got over her presence in the house, especially as a sort of guest.

'Take no notice of her. She's still feeling cross that we haven't employed her niece. She would have been totally unsuitable.'

A few moments later, Maria came back with a toast rack and a pot of coffee. She smiled sweetly at Isabel and glared once more at Stella. She smiled at Maria and said thank you very much. It had little effect.

'Really, I won't let this go on. Silly woman.'

The day passed pleasantly with a tour of the house and then they went out for lunch and did a little shopping. Soon it was time to collect the boys from school. Stella thought it seemed a long way from their home but knew it would soon become a familiar run. They were full of chatter about their day. Isabel was a good driver, despite her disabilities.

'Perhaps you would like to take the car out for a drive to familiarise yourself with it and find your way around the town a little,' Isabel suggested when they arrived back.

'Well yes, it would be a good idea but surely you'd like me to help with the boys' homework.'

'Yes, please. I want to make sure of the alphabet,' Javier piped up.

'And I've got some math to do and I need some help with that,' Juan said. 'So Stella can't go off on her own just yet.'

'Don't worry, I won't go for a while,' Stella replied with a laugh.

The usual banter for food began as soon as they got inside. Maria came out of her kitchen with a plate of cookies for them and two glasses of milk.

'We'd like some tea, please,' Isabel asked her.

'Yes, all right.' She was mumbling

something as she went out which Stella interpreted as a grumble about having to wait on her.

'Oh, dear. I'm afraid I'm not at all popular.'

When Maria came back with the tea tray, Isabel spoke to her.

'What is the problem with Stella? Why are you being so difficult?'

A torrent of Spanish came out with sideways looks at the au pair and lots of hand gestures.

'Now stop it. We speak English in this house. Your English is very good so please do not exclude Stella from the conversation by speaking in Spanish.'

'I no like her. She lazy woman. My girl she no lazy woman. She be very good with boys and help with homeworks.'

'Your niece would not be suitable, as I told you at the beginning. Her English is not very good and certainly she would never cope with dining with us every evening.'

'She eat in kitchen with me. She like

that. I like that. You should think hard about her coming instead of that English girl.' With that, she swept out of the room and slammed the door.

'Oh dear. You have it clear now,' Stella said. 'I hope she'll get over it eventually.'

'Don't worry. If she doesn't sort herself out she'll have to go. I'm sure we could find another cook who would be just as good.

'Now, you two, it's time you were doing your homework. Go and make a start and Stella will come and join you in a little while.'

They both scampered off and ran up the stairs. The two women finished their tea.

'I'm going to enjoy having you here, Stella. I think we shall become great friends.'

'Well, thank you. I think you're right.'

'I feel I've been somewhat lonely here lately. Ignacio tries hard to keep me company but he has to work so hard and has long meetings almost every day. I shall look forward to lots of chats and drives out to see something of the local countryside. I've missed that.'

Stella smiled at Isabel and touched her shoulder as she left the room. She ran up the stairs and knocked at Javier's door before opening it.

'Hello. How are you getting on?'

'I have to draw a picture of my family for my homework. Am I allowed to put you in it, too?'

'Well, I'm not sure. I'm not really a member of your family, am I?'

'But I don't want to leave you out.'

'Draw your mummy and daddy and brother and then decide. How does that sound?'

'OK.' He set to work, his tongue sticking out as he concentrated. 'Should I put Maria in?'

'If you want to.'

'But she isn't in our family, is she?'

'No. Then leave her out. I'm going to see how Juan is getting on now. See you in a few minutes.'

'All right. Then can we practise the alphabet?'

'Of course.' She smiled and went to Juan's room.

He was chewing his pen.

'How are you getting on?' Stella asked.

'Not very well. I'm stuck on my sums again. I really don't like math.'

'Funny you call it math. In England it's always plural. Maths.'

'Why?'

'I don't know. Perhaps because there are a number of them. Anyway, what is your problem?'

'I'm supposed to do division and I keep getting some left over.'

'I don't know what you're supposed to do but when I was at school we used to put an 'r' and then write the number left over. It stood for remainder.'

'Shall I try doing that?'

'If you're sure there are some left over. What numbers are you using?'

'Ninety-one divided by seven. I know that seven twelves are eighty-four so that means twelve and seven left over.'

'Think about it.'

'Oh yes. That's thirteen, isn't it?'

'It is indeed.'

'But we only go up to twelve times table.'

'Well, you're being tested a bit further. What's the next one?'

'Seventy-eight divided by six. Six into seven goes one and one left over. That makes eighteen. Six into eighteen,' he frowned a bit and then smiled. 'Three. That's thirteen again, isn't it?'

'Well done. Now you finish off while I go and take the car out for a drive. I'll see you later.'

Stella left a much happier seven-year-old boy. She still felt it was a bit much for them to have homework to the extent they did. After all, Javier was only five and for him to have to sit and do homework she felt was a bit of a strain.

Stella went down to the garage and took the keys to the small car. Inside was a box with buttons to open the garage doors. So far so good. She started the engine and once she was

58

more used to doing everything back to front in her eyes, she set off to drive out into the road.

She soon was getting the hang of it until she came to a roundabout where she drove the wrong way round it, incurring the wrath of several other drivers. Covered in blushes, she drove into what looked like a layby.

Someone drove in behind her and hooted. She was at the entrance to someone's drive. She set off again, managing to get on to the correct side of the road and drove back to the house. Heavens, she was thinking, how on earth will I ever find my way to the boys' school?

'How did you get on?' Isabel asked.

'Not all that well. I went the wrong way round a roundabout and then parked in someone's driveway. I was a disaster. I'm so frightened I'll get lost finding the school in the morning.'

'Don't worry. I'll come with you. You'll soon get used to it. The little car will soon become a friend instead of your enemy.'

'Thank you. I'd be very grateful. I know you showed me the way today but I'm not sure I can manage it yet. There's also the business of driving on the wrong side of the road.'

'Don't worry about it. You'll be fine with a bit of practice. Now, I'm wondering where Ignacio has got to. He's rather late and the boys are waiting for their dinner.'

'Where are they? I was expecting to see them.'

'In the playroom. No doubt building with Minecraft. I really can't understand the obsession with it.'

The phone rang and after Isabel had answered it, she looked somewhat grim.

'That was Ignacio. He says he'll be very late home and we should have dinner without him. I'll go and tell Maria to serve it as soon as she is ready.'

'Shall I tell the boys to come?'

'Please. Get them to wash their hands, too.' She wheeled herself towards the kitchen and pressed a remote control button on her wheelchair. The kitchen door opened and she went through.

Stella could hear her talking and she realised the housekeeper was not happy. Maria was even cross with Isabel which was not good. It seemed that things had blown up since she had arrived. Stella went to find the boys and get their hands clean ready for dinner.

'Why didn't Daddy have any dinner?' Javier asked as they finished.

'I think he had a meeting and was working late.'

'Why?'

'He just had to. Sometimes it happens. Days just aren't long enough to fit everything in.'

'Why?'

'Javier, grow up. Don't be so silly. If Dad has to work, he has to work.'

Isabel looked at her elder son gratefully. She didn't really have any answers. The little boy looked a bit tearful and Stella stepped in.

'Tell you what, I can read you a story tonight. In fact, I can tell you a story about when I was a little girl. Would you like that?'

'Oh, yes, please. That would be good, don't you think so, Mummy?'

'I think it would be excellent.' She smiled and nodded her approval.

Once they were in bed, Stella began her story.

'When I was little, I lived in a nice house with my parents. It was a long way from the village and we kept some hens and also I had a pet lamb. The hens laid eggs for us and I used to collect them every morning.'

'How may eggs did you get?' Juan asked.

'Usually only two or three. But always enough for us to have a fresh egg each most days.'

'I don't like eggs. Yuk. Nasty,' Javier said. 'What about the lamb? What did he do?'

'He was just a pet. I always wanted a dog but instead I had a lamb. He grew into quite a large sheep.'

'What did you call him?'

'He was named Woolly.'

'That's a good name for a sheep. What happened when he grew big?'

'He went away to live on a farm.'

'Did you see him after that?'

'I did for a while but then we had to move.'

Stella began to make up bits of story at this point as things became difficult for her to think about. Her father left home soon after and she and her mother needed to find a smaller place.

She made the boys laugh about the hens and one of them escaping and then one sat on eggs and they had new chicks. At last she said it was time for sleep. Juan went to his bed and settled down. She tucked both of them in and said goodnight.

In the lounge, Isabel was watching television, fortunately in English.

'No sign of Ignacio yet?'

'I've heard nothing from him. He must be tied up in a meeting.'

'That's difficult for you.'

'It's certainly unusual. He's never

63

this late but I suppose it can't be helped. Anyway, I have you here as a companion so that's something. We must get a bank sorted for you, and a card. You can't rely on having to use an English bank.'

'I suppose not. I changed money for some euros before I left so I do have some currency.'

'That's good. I'll go with you tomorrow after we've dropped the boys off.'

'Thank you. That would be good.' She yawned.

'You go to bed if you want to. I'll stay here and wait for Ignacio.'

'I don't mind waiting with you,' Stella murmured, stifling another yawn.

'You go to bed. I can see you're tired.'

'If you're sure.' Isabel nodded. 'I will then. Goodnight. See you in the morning.'

'Goodnight my dear. I'm so pleased you're here, living with us.'

So Many Hugs
and Kisses...

With very careful concentration and the occasional prompt, Stella drove to the boys' school. She gave a sigh of relief after they got out and disappeared through the gates. Phase one was over. Next she had to find the way home again.

'We'll go to the bank next,' Isabel said. 'Get you sorted. I'll pay some cash in so you can open the account.'

'But I haven't been here long enough yet to get paid.'

'No worries. I'm sure you won't abscond in the next few days.'

'Oh — I never asked, what time did Ignacio get home?'

'I'm not sure. I went to bed at midnight and he wasn't back then. He did come in at some point. I left him sleeping this morning.'

'Sorry, I wasn't being nosy.'

'Of course not. You were being a friend. A concerned friend. Thank you for that. Now, you need to turn here and there is plenty of parking outside. Would you mind getting my wheelchair out of the back, please?'

'Course. OK to stop here?'

Isabel kept her small manual chair in the boot so it was down to Stella to push her. For a moment, she experienced deja vu, remembering pushing her mother whenever they went out. Her mother did not have an electric wheelchair so she was quite used to pushing.

'Senora Mendoza,' the bank clerk greeted Isabel.

'Can we speak English, please? I'd like to introduce a friend who needs to open an account. This is Stella Lazenby, a friend over from England.'

'Welcome, Senorita. How are you liking our country?' He spoke with a strong accent but his English was good.

'I'm very happy, thank you.'

'Good. Now how can I help?'

The business was carried out quickly and efficiently and Stella came away with a publicity pack and the promise of a bank card within the next few days.

They arrived back at the house to find it empty. Ignacio had left and it was Maria's day off.

'We shall have to see what there is in the kitchen for lunch. Maria usually leaves some cold meat and salad.'

'I can sort out something when you are ready. No problem. And what about dinner this evening?'

'We usually go out on a Friday. There's a wonderful pizza restaurant in town. We usually go there.'

'Sounds brilliant. I love pizzas. We used to have them occasionally at home.'

'These are huge. The boys usually bring half of theirs home for the next day. I can never manage a whole one, either. I think Stefano will join us, too. He usually does come with us when we eat there.

'Now, I'm going to have a rest. You're free to do whatever you like for the rest of the day till we collect the boys. Oh, except for lunch. I usually eat about half past one or two o'clock.'

'I shall look forward to it. I hope I'm allowed to go into the sacred sanctuary of the kitchen. Maria was certainly not pleased when I went in the other day.'

'You're quite safe. She's gone out somewhere.'

Stella spent a happy time wandering round the garden and sitting in the warm spring sunshine. She went to sit on the terrace out of direct sunlight and picked up a book to read. She soon became engrossed and time went by rather quickly. She heard Isabel moving around and went into the kitchen to get lunch.

'Oh goodness, I'm sorry. I didn't realise it was so late.'

'Don't worry. I'm used to doing this for myself. I wasn't sure what you wanted.'

'Some of that will do fine for me,'

Stella replied, looking at the tray of cooked meat Isabel had pulled out of the fridge. 'Can I make you some salad to go with it?'

'Presumably without mayo.'

'Well, yes, not for me at least. I'm surprised you remembered that.'

'Huh. What else do I have to think about? Come on then, tuck in.'

'Thank you. It won't be long before we or I have to collect the boys.'

'I'll come with you again. I can have a rest after that. Not that I really need more rest. I fell asleep just before lunch so no problem.'

They sat together on the terrace outside and enjoyed the slight shade. Their conversation was fairly trivial and Stella tried hard to keep it that way. After all, she really didn't know the family all that well and didn't want to presume. Isabel suddenly went quiet and then taking a deep breath spoke again.

'I've got to talk to someone. I apologise about dragging you into my affairs but I'm very worried.'

'I'm sorry to hear that,' Stella mumbled, feeling slightly afraid that bad news was coming. What could it be? She was sure she hadn't done anything too wrong and wasn't about to get fired.

'It's Ignacio. I really don't know what's going on with him. I'm afraid he may have taken a mistress.'

'Oh, my goodness. No, surely not.'

'He was so late home last night and didn't really want to speak about it.'

'But he loves you and the boys. You only have to see his reaction with them. And with you . . . well, surely you feel secure with him.'

'Well in a way, yes. I'm sorry, I shouldn't be bothering you with this.'

'Please don't worry about that. I'm flattered you feel able to talk about your feelings. Don't you think it's more likely to be concerned with his business?'

'Maybe. Oh don't worry about it. It's possibly just me being silly. Finish your lunch and we'll go and collect the boys.

We can stop at the supermarket and get them a treat.'

Stella cleared their lunch things away and put them into the dishwasher. As there were so few things, she didn't turn it on and left it for when there was a full load. She went to her room and collected her bag and went down to wait for Isabel to be ready. She felt more confident driving on the wrong side of the road and handled the roundabouts with ease.

'You're getting very good,' Isabel remarked. 'I think you'll be able to manage on your own next week.'

'Thank you. I must say, I do feel more confident.'

'Look, about what I said at lunch . . . please don't repeat it, will you? In fact it was possibly just me being silly.'

'Of course I wouldn't ever repeat it.'

'You need to take the inside lane here and go into the supermarket. Buy them some nice biscuits or cookies, they call them. Get some chocolate ones. That will please them. Here, take this.' She handed a note to Stella after she had parked the car.

Stella went inside and felt bewildered at the huge range of goods but finally found the cookies. She picked up a pack she thought would do and went to the checkout.

There was a massive queue . . . typical Friday shoppers. At last she was served and left the store, apologising to Isabel when she reached the car.

'Goodness me, that was not a good time to go to the supermarket,' she remarked.

'Sorry, I should have realised. Come on now or we'll be late for the boys.'

When they arrived at the school, the two little boys were waiting, holding the hand of one of the teachers.

'I'm sorry,' Stella said. 'We stopped at the supermarket and . . . well, sorry.'

'No worry. I wait with them till you arrive. How you do. I'm Josefina. I'm teacher of Spanish to Juan.'

'How do you do.' Stella held out her hand and shook the teacher's hand.

'They good boys. I enjoy teaching Juan and look forward to teaching Javier when he come to my class next year.'

'I'm hoping to learn some Spanish myself.'

'Be good for boys to instruct you. Good luck. Bye now, boys. Enjoy your weekend.'

'Bye, Josefina. See you on Monday.'

They ran to the car and climbed in.

'How are you, Mum?' Juan asked.

'I'm fine, thank you. Had a good day?'

'Not really,' Javier said, grimacing. 'Gonzales was really mean to me at break. He told me . . . '

'He was only telling the truth,' Juan interrupted.

They drove back to the pair of the squabbling in the back. Stella concentrated on driving and didn't really listen to them. She glanced at Isabel and decided she wasn't really listening, either. She smiled and saw their mother raise her eyebrows.

'OK, you two. Enough. Talk about the good things that happened today.'

'There weren't any.' Javier slumped back in his corner and put a thumb in his mouth.

'Baby suck-a-thumb,' Juan called out.

'Now then,' Stella said sharply. 'I can't concentrate on driving with you two squabbling like that.' Silence fell and the two boys looked at each other in shock.

'You're just like everyone else. You're a grown up, too.' Juan contemplated his last statement in a sort of horror. Isabel smiled and pressed her hand on Stella's.

'Well done,' she whispered. They drove the rest of the way in almost silence.

'Stella got some cookies for you. Take your school things to your rooms and come down for them. Go on, quickly now.'

'Sorry, I didn't mean to scold them,' Stella apologised.

'I was pleased you did so. It shows you won't tolerate bad behaviour. I'm pleased about that. Perhaps you can put the biscuits on a plate and I could murder a cuppa.'

'I'll go and make one right away.'

'Thank you, dear.'

A few minutes later they were sipping their tea when Isabel spoke again.

'Please forget what I said earlier. I was having a down moment and you are right, Ignacio is obviously very fond of the boys and always seems most concerned about my welfare.'

'I've already forgotten it. Now, what time do you think we'll be going out to the pizza place?'

'About eight o'clock is usual.'

Stella smiled. One day she would get used to the seemingly late hours the family kept. She wondered how the boys coped at school as they were often not in bed much before ten.

She began to think about the evening ahead. The thought of seeing Stefano again gave her heart a sudden lurch.

Stupid girl, she was thinking. He's bound to have a girlfriend and is only

75

being polite to me because of his work. Whatever the reason, she would enjoy the company of the handsome man, she was determined.

The two boys bounced into the room and demanded their cookies.

'Wow, why can't we have them every day?' Javier demanded. 'These are so much nicer than the one Maria makes.'

'Cos they're all chocolatey and that's bad for us,' the all-knowing Juan said. 'But they are good. Can we have another?'

'You missed something out of that request,' Stella said sternly.

'Pleeeease can we have another?'

'I should think so if Mummy says it's all right.'

'One more each and then off you go to play. Stella will come and join you later when she's finished her tea.'

'OK,' Javier chirruped, grabbing his biscuit and bounding off out of the room.

'Goodness me, they seem to have so much energy.'

'Exhausting, aren't they?'

It was almost eight o'clock before Ignacio came home. He apologised to everyone and dashed off to get changed. When he came back he was as bright as ever and cheerfully asked how everyone was.

'And are we ready to show Stella our favourite pizza restaurant?'

'Yes,' the two little boys shouted in unison.

'Come on, then. Last one in the car pays the bill.' They scampered off to get in the big car first. Ignacio seemed very caring towards his wife, Stella noticed, and helped her into the car.

'Don't you need the wheelchair?' Stella asked.

'We have the one in the boot. Always keep it there.'

'Stefano? Is he meeting us at the restaurant?' Isabel asked.

'He had to see someone after work but he hopes to join us there. I hope that pleases you, Stella.'

Stella blushed a fiery red.

'Of course. It will be nice to see him again.' Her voice croaked as she spoke. She felt very embarrassed. She caught sight of Ignacio's eyes in the driving mirror. He seemed to be smiling at her as if he knew how she was feeling. Not that she really knew herself.

They parked outside the restaurant and the boys ran ahead. Ignacio took a few moments to get the wheelchair out and Isabel ensconced in it.

'You go on and make sure those two don't cause any chaos,' he said as he was helping his wife.

The two boys were in deep conversation with one of the waitresses, their arms waving and obviously both wanting to tell their story at the same time.

'Here she is. This is Stella. Stella, come and meet Yolanda. She's a friend of ours.'

'Hello,' Stella said rather shyly. 'Pleased to meet you.'

'You are lucky to have such a lovely family to work with,' Yolanda said. 'I love them all.'

'They certainly seem to have given me a huge welcome. Your English is very good.'

'I learn at school and have kept it up here as we get a lot of English people here. Now then, you two, let's take you to your table.' She led the way to a large table at one side of the room with a gap for the wheelchair. 'Is Stefano coming this evening?'

'Dunno,' Juan said. 'Probably.'

'I'll leave him a place set in case. Here are your papa and mama. I'll go get your drinks.'

'We usually have the same thing so she knows what to bring. She doesn't know what you would like.'

'I will wait for now. Come on then, let's sit down, shall we?' She noticed the waitress had stopped to speak to the parents and all were exchanging kisses and hugs. She would have to get used to the idea, she was thinking.

'Everyone all right?' Ignacio asked cheerfully. The boys both nodded and Stella smiled. 'Ah, here comes Stefano.

Come along, my boy. Sit next to Stella. That's right.'

Stefano leaned over to her and kissed her on both cheeks. Inevitably she blushed. He then shook hands with the two boys and kissed Isabel as she was parked next to him.

'How's it going?' he asked Stella.

'OK, I think. We all seem to be getting on well.'

'Of course you are. How could you not get on with these two rogues.' The boys giggled and sat back in their chairs. The drinks arrived.

'I've ordered Cava for us all. Hope you approve of that.'

'Oh yes,' Juan announced. 'Lovely.'

'Not for you, young man. For the grown ups.'

'I'm pretty well grown up. Can't I have a little?'

'When you're eighteen,' Stella said fiercely. They all laughed and the evening was off to a good start.

The males all managed to eat most of the enormous pizzas but Isabel and

Stella were totally full after eating just over half of theirs. The waitress came and removed the plates and came back moments later with cardboard boxes with the two portions of pizza the females had left over.

'Goodness, that's wonderful. I shall enjoy that for lunch tomorrow.' Stella was surprised at having it brought to her without asking.

'They always do that,' Stefano told her.

'Puddings, anyone?'

'Ice-cream,' the boys clamoured.

'Nothing for me,' Stella said. 'I'm too full, thank you.'

'In that case, may I take Stella home?' Stefano asked. 'I'd like to show her the beach along to the east first.'

'Of course,' Isabel said.

'Oh, but wouldn't you like me to help with putting the boys to bed?' Stella felt awkward about going off with Stefano.

'Don't be silly. You go and enjoy yourselves. Make sure you're back before two o'clock, however . . . I need my beauty sleep,' Ignacio joked. 'Here, let me give you a key to the house. That way it won't matter if you get in at three o'clock.'

'Goodness, I wouldn't be that late.'

'You never know. Perhaps you'll be enjoying yourself and won't want to come back to us, ever.'

'I shall show you my ancient car. I did promise you I would.'

'Well, OK then. If you're sure.'

'Of course.'

'Where are they going?' Javier asked. 'Can't we go too?'

'What? And miss out on ice-cream?'

'Couldn't they wait for us to have it first?'

'Certainly not,' Stefano said. 'My car will sulk if I don't drive it very soon.'

'You're silly,' Juan said. 'Cars can't sulk.'

'Oh, but mine can. Come on, Stella. Let's go and stop it from sulking.'

'Thank you very much for supper. I really enjoyed it,' she told her hosts. 'Be good, you two, and go to bed when you're told.'

'We will. Night, Stefano. Night, Stella. See you tomorrow.'

The two of them left the pizzeria, with Stefano stopping to say goodbye to the waitresses. He kissed them all on both cheeks while Stella stood shyly behind him.

'Goodbye, Stella. Hope we shall get to know you well,' Yolanda said. She also kissed Stella on both cheeks.

'Thank you. I hope so, too,' the English girl said.

'I don't think you are used to our custom yet, are you?' Stefano asked.

'What, all the kissing and hugging? It does seem a bit strange to me. I suppose I'll get used to it.'

'Course you will. Come on now, it's just over here.' He grabbed her hand and was almost dragging her across the road to avoid the cars speeding along. He was laughing as they arrived at his car.

'Sorry, but you have to take your

chances. Besides, it gave me a good excuse to hold your hand.'

'And you really need an excuse?' she teased.

'Well, you're a well-brought-up English girl. I don't know what you expect with us hot blooded Spaniards.'

'But I thought you were half English.'

'Well, yes, but I live in Spain.' His eyes twinkled and his smile was broad.

Stella was enchanted by this handsome young man who seemed to be showing such an interest in her. It was a complete surprise to her. She had scarcely ever exchanged words with someone of the opposite sex, let alone spent time alone with one of them.

She needed to be careful, she realised. Someone like Stefano could never be serious about her. Someone as good-looking and personable as him, must have a girlfriend or two.

'Are you sure about this?' she asked.

'What? Taking you for a drive? Of course I am. It's my privilege that you're even interested in coming with me. Mind you, thinking about it, I didn't give you much of a chance to refuse.'

She gave a giggle.

'I could have said no. I wanted to come. But I hope I'm not keeping you from your girlfriend.'

'Oh? And what girlfriend is that?'

'I just thought you must have one. Or two.'

'And when do you think I have time? I work very hard, often into the late evenings. You are the first girl I've even spent time with lately.'

'I presumed that was partly because of the Mendoza family. I thought you were being polite because of them.'

'Don't put yourself down, Stella. You are a lovely person. You must get lots of attention here with that beautiful hair and eyes. Worth a fortune in Spain. You need to sit on the other side of the car, unless you want to drive of course.'

'Oh, silly me. Of course. I'll get used to it eventually I'm sure.' She went round to the other side and got in. 'I thought you said you had an old wreck of a car? This seems very smart and not at all a wreck.'

'Perhaps I exaggerated a little. In comparison to Ignacio's car, it is a virtual wreck.'

They set off. The road seemed to go on for ever. Stella hadn't been along the beach front since she'd arrived and she looked around with interest. Several bars were lit up, with crowds of people inside, and some were almost empty. A number of people were strolling along at the side of the road.

'Goodness, I had no idea it was such a large town here. Why are some bars so full and others are almost empty?'

'If they knew that, no doubt the owners would change things. I suppose it's a case of being popular or not.' They came to the end and carried on driving along the coast. At times they were close to the sea and at others they seemed to be inland, driving among high rocky sides to the road, using the headlights to show them.

'Where are we going?' Stella asked after they had driven for several kilometres.

'There's a little beach a bit further along. You can get a view back along at the town. You'll love it, I'm sure.' Stefano drove down a narrow track and stopped at what looked like the edge of the sea. 'Look along there. See all the lights?'

'Oh, wow, yes. It looks very pretty.' She opened the car door and got out. It was a sandy beach and she walked over it towards to sea. She slipped her sandals off and paddled in the tiny waves as they washed on the shore. 'Come on. It's warm.'

'No way. Watch out for jellyfish. There are some in the area and they will sting you.'

'Oh, no. I hate them!' She ran out of the water and went back to him. 'Are there really jellyfish?'

'No, but I wanted you to come out of the water. Come here, Stella.' He held out his arms and she almost fell into them. She was still holding her sandals and she almost hit him with them.

'Put them down and come here,' he ordered. She dropped them and went into his arms. 'I've been longing to do this since I first met you.' Stefano kissed her fully on the lips. Stella kissed him back with enthusiasm.

'Excuse me asking but I don't think you've done that too many times in the past.'

'How do you know?'

'Oh, I'm not sure. It felt as if you were experiencing it for the first time.'

'You must be quite an expert if you could tell all that. I'm ready to go back now. I don't want to be too late getting home.'

'Oh, Stella, Stella. I'm sorry. I wasn't . . . Please stay a while longer. Tell me about yourself. Your life and what you've been doing. Please.'

'Let's sit down, then.' They sat on a rock at one side of the beach and she asked him what he wanted to know.

'All about you and your life till now.'

'I did my A-levels and then left school. I'd hoped to go to university but had to give that up when my mother became ill.'

'That's sad.'

Stella nodded.

'She used to manage on her own for most of the day so I worked. Nothing too exciting, just a shop. I had to do everything when I got home. Including getting her meals ready for the next day after I'd cooked dinner for that night.'

'For how long did all this go on?'

'About seven years. She became ill while I was doing my exams. Poor Mum. She tried hard not to be a problem to me.' She fell silent and sat for a while. Stefano sat quietly holding her hand and waiting for her to continue.

'You all right?'

'Yeah. Can't really be upset about her end. She really wanted it to end. She was in such pain it was a great relief when she did die.'

'I'm so sorry.'

'It's all right. Thank you anyway. Now, enough of the morbid stuff. I'm starting my new life here in Spain. Loving it so far. Oh, except for Maria.'

'Maria? Is she still giving you a hard time?'

Stella nodded.

'She hates me. Mostly because I'm English but I took the job she wanted for her niece. She tells me, 'You lazy woman.' Stella sighed. 'I can cope with a few insults. She'll get used to me.'

'I hope so. Now, shall we get back to where we were earlier? I was quite enjoying it.'

She smiled and blushed in the darkness, glad that he couldn't see her red cheeks. He put his arm round her shoulders and gently turned her towards him. She gave a sigh of pure pleasure. If she was being foolish, she didn't care.

Her life had been one of always being careful not to be out late and always looking after her mum. Rarely had she gone out in the evenings with friends and now, suddenly, she was a free agent. Free to enjoy herself and free to see whoever she wanted to see.

At the moment, it was Stefano. As he kissed her, she melted into his arms and would have been quite happy to stay exactly where she was for ever. She lost track of the time and even of where she was.

At last, Stefano spoke.

'I think it must be time to take you home, Miss Lazenby. You may have a key but you have to get up in the morning.'

'Goodness me, it's past midnight. Please, take me home quickly. I never go to bed this late.'

His Other Woman

It was a hot night and Stella tossed and turned and didn't manage to fall asleep till very late. All too soon, she heard the two boys shouting at each other and then roaring with laughter. Quickly, she dressed and went to see what they were up to.

'What's all the noise about?' she asked severely.

'Nothing. We're just having fun. Javie's an idiot and being silly.'

'No, I'm not. I just put my pants on my head and that made him laugh.'

'Well, I suggest you put them in the proper place and we'll go and see about breakfast.'

'Did you have a nice time last night?' Juan asked her.

'I did, thank you.'

'Where did you go?' Javier was curious.

'Just along the playa. We stopped at a little beach at the other end.'

'What? You didn't go to a bar and start dancing?' Javier started performing a silly dance standing on his bed.

'Certainly not. Come on then. Get dressed and come through.'

'We don't have to get dressed on a Saturday. We sometimes go straight into the pool and it's not worth it.'

'Really?' she said incredulously. 'I don't know if you're having me on or being genuine.'

'He's having you on. But we don't have to wear our uniforms. Yeah! Mummy lets us choose what we wear.'

'OK, then. I'll believe you. But hurry up.'

Stella went down and looked into the dining-room. The table was laid for breakfast and she wondered whether she should say anything to Maria. She decided against risking another confrontation and wandered into the lounge and looked out of the window.

The sea was sparkling and lots of small boats were already out sailing. Some larger boats seemed to be out there fishing and powering along the coast to the harbour of the next village. She heard a noise and turned to see who was there. It was Maria.

'Why you standing there doing nothing? You should be with boys, helping them to dress. You lazy woman.'

'They can manage to dress themselves,' Stella retorted. 'Their parents like them to be independent.'

'You still lazy lazy woman. You don't get home till all hours . . . out enjoying yourself with men, no doubt.'

'Not that it has anything to do with you, but I was out with a friend of the family with their permission and knowledge.' Stella had become quite red in the face as she was feeling so angry.

'Won't last long here. You go back England very soon.' With that Maria swept out of the room and went back to the kitchen.

Stella stood still for a few moments longer, determined she was not going to be beaten by that woman, as she thought of her. Isabel came along and into the room.

'Is everything all right? I thought I heard raised voices.'

'Nothing really. It's all right.'

'Did you enjoy yourself last evening?'

'I really did. Thank you again for the pizzas.'

'Our pleasure. And how was Stefano?' 'Fine, thank you. He was polite as always. We talked a lot.'

'Did he tell you anything about his background?'

'Well no, not really.' Stella thought back on their conversation and realised she had done most of the talking. 'I think I talked to him mostly. Telling him about my background. How dreadful of me. I never even asked much about him.' She blushed once more at the memory, partly at the memory of his kisses and also about her own failure to ask him anything.

'Is there something I should know?' she asked.

'I leave it to him to tell you when he's ready.'

'Now you've got me intrigued. I hope he isn't the son of someone who's done dreadful things.'

'Of course not. We wouldn't welcome him into the house if he was. Now, are the boys coming through for breakfast?'

'I'll check on them. They should be ready by now.' She went through to the stairs and called out to them. They came running down, dressed in brightly coloured shorts and T-shirts, looking like typical, lively little boys.

They both ran to their mother and kissed her on both cheeks then they sat down at the table. Their mother offered them fruit and cereal which they ate with relish.

'Stella, help yourself to whatever you feel like. Maria will bring toast and coffee through in a moment. Now, what do you want to do today, boys?'

'Go in the pool. And maybe go out

with Stella to show her the town.'

'If she would like that. How do you feel about being shown the town by these two?'

'That would be lovely. I saw lots of places as we drove along the playa yesterday but I haven't been into any of the shops or anything. Oh, apart from when you took me the other day.'

Maria came in and dumped the coffee pot on the table. She put toast in front of Isabel and glared at Stella.

'Maria? What is wrong?'

She shook her head and then babbled something in Spanish. Isabel glanced at the girl and shook her head. She said something back to her in Spanish and both boys also turned to stare at Stella, their eyes wide in disbelief.

'Have I done something wrong?' Stella asked anxiously.

'I don't think so. She said you'd been rude to her. But I can't really believe that.'

'I'm sorry, but she was rude to me. I did tell her I was out with your permission and with a friend of the family.'

'Nothing more?'

'I don't think so.'

'Nothing about her being lazy?'

'Of course not. She accused *me* of being a lazy . . . ' She paused, not wanting to get the woman into trouble. 'She clearly doesn't like me but I would never be rude to her.'

'Very well. That's good enough for me. Now, would you like some coffee?'

'Thank you.'

'Perhaps she's put poison in it. She wants to get rid of this English girl,' Juan said.

'Don't be silly, Juan,' his mother admonished him. 'I don't like you making such comments. Have some toast and some of the jam you like.'

'Yes, please,' he said enthusiastically.

They planned their morning and decided to go swimming after the trip out to the town. They decided to walk to the shops along the playa, rather than drive. Once they had finished their breakfast, the boys went to clean their teeth and put on their sweaters. Almost leaping around, they set out to walk to the shops.

'Mummy has given us some euros to spend,' one of them told her. 'I'm going to buy a magazine.'

'I'm going to buy sweets,' the other said.

'Let's see. Perhaps you'll change your mind when we get there. Come on then. Let's go.'

They walked along the road with the two boys bouncing along, both of them chattering at once. Stella tried hard to hang on to their hands but it wasn't easy. She almost dragged them past a souvenir shop loaded with all manner of tacky things, suggesting there were more interesting places for them to spend their euros.

'But we really, really want to go in there. They have all sorts of interesting things inside.'

'Perhaps one day you can go with your father.'

'He'd never let us go in there,' Juan protested. 'He says it's all rubbish.'

'Precisely,' Stella said primly.

Javier began to sulk. His lip trembled and she realised he was only a very little boy, despite his sophisticated demeanour.

'Hey, it's all right. Come on, let's go and find a shop that sells magazines and papers.'

'There's one along here,' Javier told her. 'Actually, it's next to the ice-cream shop.' They both looked up at her as if willing her to react. 'We are allowed ice-creams sometimes,' he added.

'But it's not long since you had breakfast.' Stella laughed.

'It'll be ages before lunch, though,' Juan said.

'We'll see. Maybe I'll buy you an ice-cream if you're very good.'

'Oh we are,' Javier replied promptly.

'Look, there's Stefano,' Juan said, slipping her hand and running over to him.

'Hey, come back here,' she called uselessly.

Stefano looked slightly embarrassed. They walked towards him.

'Hi,' she said.

'Hello. I see you have the two rascals with you.'

'We were just thinking of having an ice-cream. Would you like to join us?' Stella invited.

'I'm sorry but I'm . . . well, in a hurry.' He kept looking around him as if he was anxious about something.

'No worries. We don't want to delay you.'

'No, it's OK. I'm just . . . never mind. I really do have to go now. Sorry. Bye. I did enjoy last night,' he added hurriedly as he dashed into the shop.

Stella saw him speak to someone who had their back towards her and realised it was a female. She gulped. He was with a woman and didn't want them to see her. Oh well, she could hardly have expected him to be on his own and exclusive to her all the time, now could she?

'Come on then, boys, let's go and see

what sort of ice-cream they have in this shop.'

'Every sort. What's your favourite?'

'Coffee. But I don't expect they have that. Not many places do.'

'Yes, they do.' Javier nodded enthusiastically. 'I know they do.'

'Let's go in and see then, shall we?'

The two little boys dashed into the shop and stood gazing into the large freezer.

They were pointing excitedly and both talking at the same time about which flavours they wanted. Stella stood back and watched as Stefano led the woman he was with along the road. He put his arm round her as they walked and she felt gutted. How could she ever have imagined she could attract him?

With something of a sigh, she followed the boys into the ice-cream shop and tried to show enthusiasm. Soon, they were all licking their cones as they wandered out into the street.

'Let's go and sit down in front of the

sea,' Stella suggested. They crossed the road and found a seat. Once the ice-creams had been eaten, the boys wanted to run down to the sea and they spent a happy few minutes on the beach.

'Let's go and see what you want to buy, shall we?' she suggested.

'Oh, yes, please. Come on, Juan.'

'Wait a moment. You mustn't run across the road. Stop and look out for moving traffic.' Obediently, they stopped at the edge and took her hands. It took a while for them to decide how to spend their money but at last, decisions were made and they went out of the shop clutching their purchases.

They were soon back at their home. Ignacio was sitting reading his paper and lifted his head.

'Had a good walk?'

'Yes thank you, Papa. Stella bought us ice-creams. She likes coffee best, like Mama.'

'So soon after breakfast? But that was kind of her.'

'We saw Stefano, too. He was busy though so he didn't come with us to the ice-cream place. Can we go swimming now?' Juan asked.

'Where do you guys get your energy from?' Ignacio asked. 'Give me five minutes more with my paper and then I'll come with you.'

'I don't mind taking them,' Stella offered. 'I used to enjoy swimming before . . . well, when I was at school.'

'Great, well, go and change, boys.'

The boys scampered off to their rooms only to return seconds later clad in bathing trunks.

'Ready,' Javier said. 'Why haven't you changed, Stella?'

'I'm just going.' She ran up the stairs to her room and quickly changed. Somehow, she had to get used to the idea that Stefano had another girl-friend. She felt slightly embarrassed that she had kissed him with such enthusiasm but it was too late now for regrets.

'Come on, Stella. We've been waiting

for hours and hours.'

'Go on with you. Two minutes at the most.' They went down the stairs to the next floor and into the pool area. It was very warm in there and very blue. 'Oh goodness, I never thought about towels. We don't want to go back upstairs dripping.' Both boys laughed.

'We have towels down here. And a shower. They are special towels for swimming.'

Seconds later, they both dived into the water and were yelling at each other in great excitement. Stella stepped on to the steps and lowered herself into the water carefully. It was blissfully warm, about the temperature she would have had a bath at home.

She swam a length of breaststroke and realised the pool was quite deep at the far end. She swam back and asked the boys how well they could swim, feeling slightly worried about them getting so out of their depth. She didn't need to worry at all. They both swam like fishes and though they splashed a lot, were quite safe. Ignacio arrived sporting his swimming trunks.

'Where are you two crabs?' he asked. 'I can only see a mermaid.'

'We're here ready to nip you, Daddy.' They both swam towards him nipping their fingers together.

'Ouch,' he yelled, grabbing them under his arms. 'Only one way to deal with naughty crabs,' he said and threw them into the water away from him. 'And how is the mermaid getting on?'

'Fine, thank you. It's wonderful in here.'

'No chlorine. It's a pool run on salt which makes its own chlorine. I don't really understand it but that's what they tell me. I'm going to swim a few lengths now. Come on, you two, swim alongside me.'

Obediently the two boys started to swim beside their father. He was an excellent swimmer and soon left them behind, puffing along in the warm blue water.

Stella took over the routine and

swimming more slowly, they kept up with her. She wasn't a bad swimmer and was soon back in her own routine, her lengths getting faster as she swam up and down.

The two boys soon tired of swimming and wanted to play. Javier collected a large blow up ball and started to biff it towards his brother. He hit it back and soon there was a competition starting.

Ignacio organised them into two teams and they started an hilarious game of chase. At last he laughed and told them he was getting too old for such activities.

'Come on, out you two. Have a shower and get dried. It must be lunch time.'

The two boys raced off to have their shower and soon came out wrapped in colourful towels. They went upstairs and left Stella with Ignacio.

'You go and shower,' Ignacio said to Stella. 'There are towels in the shower room. Help yourself.'

'Thanks. I won't be long.' She took her shower and wrapped herself in a towel just as the boys had done. She left her costume in the basket provided, along with the boys' trunks. Perhaps she would come back later and rinse them through.

Back in her room she soon dressed and went back into the lounge. She wondered what there would be for lunch as she was feeling rather peckish. Perhaps she would have her pizza leftover from last night.

Thinking of that made her remember her time with Stefano. She even blushed at the memory. Why ever had she been so enthusiastic? Why had she kissed him with such confidence? She shook her head.

'Oh, there you are,' Isabel said as she wheeled herself into the room. 'Enjoyed your swim?'

'Yes, thank you. It's a lovely pool.'

'I do agree. I go in myself at times but it's a bit of a business. We have a sort of hoist which I can use. I tend to go in when the boys are at school. Tell me, what's the matter?'

'Er, nothing. Not really.'

'You weren't listening to me. I think there is something wrong. You can tell me.'

'Nothing, really. I just made a fool of myself last night and now I'm regretting it. Bitterly regretting it.'

'With Stefano?'

'Well, yes. I was stupid. I shouldn't ever have behaved like that.'

'But he's lovely. Almost like one of the family. I can't imagine what you think you've done wrong.'

Maria came into the room and interrupted the two females.

'Lunch is served. I've put it on the terrace outside. It's a nice day and fresh air will do you good.'

'Thank you, Maria. Very thoughtful of you. Would you mind calling the boys, Stella?'

'Of course not. Will Ignacio join us too?'

'Oh, yes. He's probably playing some

computer game with them. Try there first.'

Stella left the room and went in search of the boys. Maria turned to Isabel and spoke to her.

'She no good that one. You need to know she no come home till verrry late. She out with boys. Note my words. She lazy woman. Say so before. She not look after boys properly.'

'Now, Maria, you don't know that.'

'I do know. I hear her come in very late.'

'I know she stayed out after we came home. We gave her a key so it wasn't a problem. And I really don't like you using that phrase. We are very pleased to have her here.'

'But my niece, she good girl. She no cost as much.'

'We've discussed this, Maria. Several times. Your niece cannot speak English very well.' She gave a sigh.

'But she willing to learn. She take lessons.'

'That's the end of it. Stella is here

and is staying for as long as she wants to. Now, if you can't accept it, then perhaps you should look for another job.'

Maria went out of the room swearing in a Spanish that even Isabel couldn't recognise. She gave a sigh. Why was nothing simple?

A Spiteful Act

The family spent a quiet weekend at home, the boys playing on their computers and other games. Stella played junior monopoly with them, cheating madly to help them win. Ignacio was working in his study and Isabel sat reading the papers.

After lunch, they told Stella she could go out and explore the area if she wanted to. She wasn't too keen on going out on her own but decided it would be good for her to get to know the region. Ignacio suggested he might take the boys out to the park and she was free for the rest of the day.

It still felt strange to her to drive on the wrong side of the road but it was getting better. She rather wished Stefano was with her, chatting the way he did and making her laugh. She had known him for less than a week and felt she was becoming obsessed with him.

It was so wrong of her. He obviously had a girlfriend and was spending his weekend with her. Lucky her, she was thinking rather sadly.

She must snap out of it. Stefano was a family friend and because he worked for Ignacio, he was merely being polite to her as a newcomer. All the same, he had certainly been more than friendly on Friday night. She drove past the little beach which had so many memories for her and continued driving inland for a while.

She was starting to climb and realised she had driven quite a long way. Perhaps it was time to turn around and go back towards the town. She spotted a wide drive and decided to use that as a turning point. As she did so, lights flashed and the large gates opened. Goodness me, she was thinking. Whatever have I done? A large car was coming towards her and she panicked, managing to stall the engine.

'Sorry,' she called out through the

window. An angry face glared at her and she vaguely heard a torrent of angry sounding Spanish.

'*No hablo español*,' she managed to mutter.

'Get away from here. This not a turning place,' came back to her.

'Sorry,' she called again, this time managing to start the car and move forward, almost hitting the large car that loomed in front of her. She braked and then put it into reverse, backing out of the drive and into the road, where another car was coming. He hooted angrily but managed to stop.

Stella was very close to tears but she fought against it and finally managed to drive on. She was shaking all over and any smattering of confidence she'd had disappeared.

She finally parked the car on a rough bit of ground to one side of the road. She got out and stood looking at the scenery. There were distant glimpses of the sea and towering cliffs of rock on the other side. If she wasn't feeling so awful, she might have noticed how lovely it looked. After a few minutes, she felt calmer again and was ready to go back to the house.

Driving a little more sedately, she was soon back in the town and despite there being a lot more traffic, she managed to get back without further adventures.

She saw a car parked outside the house and wondered who was visiting. She was surprised to see it was Stefano.

'I didn't recognise your car. Hello there.' Stella's knees were knocking slightly at the sight of him.

'I was just about to go away when I saw nobody was at home. I'm so glad you came back when you did. Have you been out for a drive?'

'Well, yes, of course. Ignacio and Isabel must have taken the boys out.'

'They usually do something on a Sunday. I thought you might also like a drive out.'

'I thought you'd be spending time with your girlfriend.'

'Girlfriend? I don't have a girlfriend.'

'The one you were with yesterday in the town. I saw you together.' He laughed.

'She'd be flattered you thought she was my girlfriend. She's my older sister. She has a disability and I usually take her out shopping on a Saturday.'

'Oh, I see,' Stella said, beginning to shake again. She felt so relieved she could hardly believe it.

'So where is she now?'

'With my mother. She looks after Noelia most of the time, except when she goes to her work unit. But, are we going out for a drive or not?'

'Yes, please. Let me put the car away and then we can go.'

Soon they were speeding along the roads leading along the coast in the other direction. Stella wondered if she would ever have the confidence to drive the way Stefano did.

'Tell me about Noelia.'

'She's a Down's syndrome person. She's just over thirty and manages fairly well. She goes to a work unit most mornings, which gives my mum a break. Noelia's pretty bright actually, reads and writes well and enjoys her work.'

'And your mum? How does she cope?'

'She has problems with arthritis.'

'Oh, goodness me.'

'We manage. I'm lucky to have a well-paid job and so we don't have problems with money. We own the house we live in, so all is well.'

Stella thought about his words. Obviously he was very important to his mother and sister. What would happen if he wanted his own independence? Wisely, she didn't make any comment on that subject.

Stella well knew the problems of being a carer after looking after her own mother for so long. She had always put her mother first though her mother had often told her to go out in the evenings. Strangely, she had never really wanted to leave her, just in case anything went wrong.

'Penny for them.' Stefano smiled.

'Nothing really. Where are we going?'

'Just a little way along the coast. There's a pretty fishing village I thought you might like.'

'Sounds nice. Does Noelia like to go out with you?'

'She only wants to go to the shops. I do take both of them out sometimes but Mum doesn't really like it and Noelia gets very distressed if she's out of her comfort zone.'

'That's difficult for you.'

'Not really. I'm used to it.' Stella heard his words and felt rather sad for him. Still, the Mendoza family possibly made up for it as best as they could.

'Ignacio and Isabel do look after us pretty well. I get excellent pay which is how we managed to buy our house.'

'They do seem to be a lovely couple. I adore their two boys. So full of fun and both of them are so obedient. Not a bit typical of English boys of that age.'

'Nor Spanish ones,' Stefano said. 'Usually they are real tykes. I do like that word. Tykes.'

Stella laughed.

'You are funny. Where did you learn that one? As far as I know it doesn't usually come into language classes.'

'I spent some time in Yorkshire when I was at university. I did a year in the UK to update on computer ideas. The family I stayed with had a couple of tykes and so I learned the word. Mind you, they were very naughty and made their parents cross with them.'

Stella giggled again.

'Here we are. I'll find somewhere to park and we'll take a walk.'

It was a very pretty village in a Spanish way. Not quite like the Cornish fishing villages she was used to. The boats looked different but she couldn't quite work out why. As it was low tide, they were all moored alongside the quay.

'I wonder why the boats look different from Cornish boats.'

'Different styles for different purposes, I suppose. Perhaps it's the sort of

119

fish they catch or maybe the conditions they go out in.'

They chatted on for a while and eventually sat down overlooking the harbour. It was very pleasant in the sunshine and Stella began to feel dozy. Stefano slipped his arm round her shoulders almost to support her.

Instantly she lost her sleepy feelings and felt stirred. He leaned over and kissed her. She responded immediately and then felt slightly ashamed, sitting there in full view of everyone walking round.

'Sorry, it's just a bit public here. Let's walk a bit more.'

Hand in hand, they set off along the side of the harbour. Stefano stroked the hand he held, sending waves of something she scarcely recognised through her whole body. She almost felt scared by them.

She tried to tell herself it was simply because she had never had anyone this close to her before. She really hoped she wasn't getting caught in some weird sort of trap but somehow, she couldn't believe it of the man. She really wanted to enjoy his attention and not spoil anything.

'You've gone very quiet,' he said at last. 'Something wrong?'

'No, not really.' Stella shook her head. 'I'm just having thoughts . . . about us.'

'Us? What do you mean.'

'Oh, I'm just being silly. Forget about it. Perhaps we should go back now. The family may have returned and will want some help getting the boys to bed.'

'No, please tell me. Have I done something wrong?' He looked so woebegone she almost laughed.

'Of course you haven't. You're always the perfect gentleman.'

'So why are you looking so concerned?'

'I'm probably being very naive but you do seem to be very friendly and I'm . . . well, I'm just not used to it. We don't know each other very well and I . . . ' she faltered.

'Oh Stella, my dear Stella. Don't you realise you're a very beautiful lady. Of course I'm going to be friendly towards you and much more than friendly, I hope. Of course it's early days yet.

'But I want to get to know you better and better. In fact if you hadn't said you want to go home, I was going to suggest I take you to my home. You could meet my sister and my mother. How does that sound to you?'

'Really? I'd like that very much. But do we have time?'

'What did the Mendozas say to you before they left? Did they ask you to get back to help them?'

'Well, no. I just thought they'd like it if I was there.'

'Possibly they might. But please, come back with me and meet my family.'

'OK. Let's do that,' she agreed shyly. She felt uncertain about his reasons for asking her to accompany him and nervous about meeting his mother.

'Will they mind a stranger suddenly turning up?'

'Not at all. They'll be pleased to see who I'm spending my time with.'

They drove a short way through the town and up towards the higher part amongst a group of houses that all looked neat and trim but still very Spanish. He stopped outside one of them.

'This is our place. Welcome.'

'Thank you. It looks very nice.'

'We like it. Not too big to look after and an easy garden for me. OK. You ready?' She nodded and got out of the car. It was a steep slope leading up to the house. She wondered how his mother coped with that.

'This is a bit steep. Mum finds it a bit tricky walking down it but she doesn't need to go out all that much.'

'I was wondering. How about your sister? Noelia.'

'She doesn't go outside the gates on her own so it isn't a problem.'

They walked to the door and he took

out keys to open it.

'Hi there, you two. I've brought someone to see you.'

'Come in. Who have you brought to see us?' came the voice of a female. They went into a large, light room overlooking a pretty garden which actually looked quite English except for a few exotic flowers.

'I'd like you to meet Stella. She's working for the Mendoza family and as this is her first visit to Spain, I'm showing her some of the sights.'

'Pleased to meet you, my dear.'

'And I you. And this must be Noelia. How are you today?' The girl smiled at her and held out her hand.

'Hello. I like your dress,' she said. 'You've got pretty hair.'

'Well, thank you,' Stella replied, slightly taken aback by the girl's directness.

'You're obviously 'in' with our Noelia,' Stefano laughed. 'She doesn't take to everyone.'

'Do sit down, my dear. Would you

like some tea? Or perhaps a cold drink?'
His mother was charming. She had
light brown curly hair and brown eyes
and a ready smile.

Stella could see some likeness with
Stefano but his Latin looks possibly
owed more to his father.

'I'd like something cold, please. I'm
not really used to the heat yet and seem
to spend most of my time looking for
cold drinks.'

'Can you get some for us all,
Stefano?'

'Would you like a beer? Or some
revolting stuff that Noelia likes.'

'Perhaps I'll go for beer, thanks,' she
replied. He disappeared through a door
that presumably led to the kitchen. She
heard the clink of glasses, water
running and then he came back.

'Sorry, Mum, I didn't ask you what
you wanted.'

'I'll have a beer as well.'

'Just as well — that's what I brought
for you.'

'I want my juice,' Noelia wailed.

125

'Don't like beer.'

'There it is, then. Aren't I clever to have guessed that?'

'Yes, you are clever, Stefano. That's just what I wanted.' She drank it straight down in one go, handed him the container and remarked it had been nice.

'So, what do you do for the Mendoza family? I presume you work at the house rather than the factory,' his mother said.

'I help Mrs Mendoza with the boys. It's a lovely place and the boys are delightful. I think I have a perfect job.'

'You are very lucky. They are a good family and have been good to us.'

The conversation went on with them talking about the town and what they all liked to do. It seemed that Noelia went off to her little job most mornings and Mrs Sanchez rested, ready for the afternoon when she looked after her daughter.

'My name is Joanne. Please call me that. I don't like being formal,'

Stefano's mother said.

'That sounds very English.' Stella laughed. 'I don't know why but I expected you would have a Spanish name.'

'Goodness me, no, I am English and proud of it. They pronounce it in the Spanish way of course with a sort of 'h' sound at the start of it. My late husband insisted on Spanish names for the children.'

At last, Stella noticed the time.

'Goodness me, I need to get back. The family will be wondering where I am. Thank you for your hospitality and I'm so pleased to have met you.'

'Do come again, please. I've really enjoyed our conversation and meeting you. I hope you'll be very happy here in Spain.'

'Thank you. I will certainly look forward to seeing you both again.'

They drove back to the Mendozas' home, which didn't seem too far away.

'I didn't realise you're almost a neighbour,' she remarked.

'Not quite in the same league. Still, at least our home belongs to us which is almost remarkable for someone of my age.'

'I'll say it is. There would be no chance of you owning your own house in the UK. Prices are quite scary, especially in London. We only rented our place even in Cornwall. It was all I could do to keep us in there. Still, that's all in the past now. I own nothing and have nowhere to go if I leave here.'

'Hopefully that gives you an incentive to stay, then.'

'Do you want to come in and say hello?'

'Yes, please. I need a word with Ignacio anyway. It'll save me having to phone him.'

Stella used her key to open the door and she called out that she was back. Isabel was in the lounge.

'Had a nice time?' she asked.

'Lovely, thank you. I've brought Stefano in. He wanted to see Ignacio.'

'I'm glad to see you. Would you like a

drink? Help yourself. We're going to eat when Ignacio comes back. He's putting the boys to bed. Stay and eat with us. It's only a light supper.'

'Well, thanks. Can I pour you something?'

'I'll have a white wine please. What about you, Stella?'

'Same for me. Thanks.'

Stefano was obviously used to pouring drinks for everyone and did it swiftly. He handed glasses to the two women and poured a beer for himself.

'Sorry, I didn't mean to gatecrash your evening,' he said.

'Don't be silly. We're always pleased to see you. Where have you been?'

'Along the coast to Villaricos. We had a walk round there. Then I took Stella to meet Mum and Noelia.'

'Oh, that was nice. I expect they were pleased to see her.'

'They were,' Stella agreed. 'Lovely lady and Noelia is very sweet. I didn't realise they live so close to here. I say, should I go and help Ignacio? Perhaps he'd like to come in here.'

'Goodness me, no. He would hate anyone going to help him. This is his special time with his sons. Thank you for the thought anyway. He won't be much longer.'

Stella settled down again and relaxed. Stefano came to sit beside her. Isabel noticed and gave a small smile.

'I can see you two are getting on well. That's lovely.'

Stella blushed and Stefano grinned from ear to ear.

'You are a shrewd lady, Isabel. It is still early days but we seem to be getting on very well, aren't we?' Stella nodded, still a fiery red. Fortunately, Ignacio came in at this point.

'Excellent. We have nice company. You will stay to eat with us, won't you? Of course you will. Now, have you all got drinks? All except me.'

'Can I pour something for you?' Stefano offered.

'I can manage it. Anyone need topping up? Those two rogues needed a firm hand. I hope you can cope with them, Stella. They are totally wicked.'

'Really?' she said incredulously.

'Terrible, they are.'

'Ignacio, stop teasing us. You know you adore them both. They can twist you round their fingers. How many stories have you read to them tonight?'

'Only two, well, perhaps three. Or was it four? I don't know. Has anyone told Maria about supper?'

'I wasn't sure when you'd be ready. I'll go and tell her now.' Isabel moved her wheelchair towards the kitchen and pressed the button to open the door. She disappeared through it and came back a few minutes later.

'She'll bring it in right away. Her niece was in there with her. I really don't like that girl. I'm so glad we didn't employ her.'

'I think I'm glad you didn't, either,' Stella said. 'Otherwise I wouldn't be here and wouldn't know any of you. I think I would have missed a lot of good things.'

Maria came in with a series of plates and dishes.

'I fetch soup now,' she said and left the room. She returned with a large tureen and ladle and put it down on the table. Come while it hot.' She turned to leave the room. 'My niece is here. She want to bring food in so you see her useful.'

'Thank you, Maria.'

'A narrow escape,' Ignacio said. 'Come on then, everyone, let's eat.'

It was delicious soup and everyone had second helpings. There was cooked meat and salad to follow and a tarte au citron after that. Stella thought she might burst if she ate any more.

Once the meal was finished, Stefano went off with Ignacio into his study. Isabel and Stella went to sit down.

'Should I clear the table?' Stella asked.

'No. Maria will do it when she's ready. I think she's chatting to her niece and probably won't do it till she goes.'

'Excuse me for a moment. I need to

go to my room to fetch my phone,' Stella said. She went upstairs and into her bedroom. She gasped at what she saw. All her clothes were strewn around on the floor. She had left it perfectly tidy with everything put in the wardrobe. Who on earth had done this? Angrily, she picked things up and laid them on the bed. She felt tears forming. Who on earth hated her so much? Maria's niece. She instinctively knew it had been her.

She sat down and wondered if she should say something to Isabel. She had every right to do so but she decided to keep quiet about it. It would do no good to alienate Maria even more, assuming she even knew about this latest catastrophe. She decided to bide her time. She would get her own back one day before long. She went downstairs again and Isabel looked at her.

'Everything all right?' she asked.

'Fine, thanks.'

Serious Problem

The two men seemed to be ensconced in Ignacio's study for some time. Stella sat yawning, wondering if she might go to bed but she wanted to say goodnight to Stefano. She kept thinking about the mess in her room and knew she would have to sort it out before she could even contemplate getting into her bed.

'Do you want to see the television?' Isabel asked.

'We might as well. Not sure if I'll be able to understand it, mind you.'

'It's all right. We have satellite anyway. But you know that. Make sure that's what you put on.'

Stella got up and fiddled with the remote until she found the right channel. It was the news. She sat down and listened to various events round the world. She suddenly felt very remote from it all.

Her life was almost cut off from all the problems. The most she had to think about was looking after two little boys. She felt slightly guilty as before she left England, she had done some voluntary work for a group of ecologists. She really did care about recycling and the future of the planet.

'I ought to see if there's somewhere here that is fighting the use of plastic,' she muttered.

'Sorry,' Isabel said. 'I didn't catch what you said.'

'I was just thinking about plastic. Have you seen the amount of plastic we use in our lives? It's frightening. I mean how much of it do we recycle?'

'Not much at all. Maria doesn't believe in it. Besides, it makes extra work for her and she doesn't like that. I feel I can't demand that she does recycle anything.' Stella thought for a few minutes.

'It might be complicated but perhaps I could sort it out. What do you think?'

'I don't think you should. You know

how she feels about you being in this house. It could get very complicated if you invaded her kitchen. Goodness me, it's bad enough if I go in there.' They both laughed. At this point the men emerged from the study.

'Can I get you a drink?' Ignacio offered.

'Not for me, thanks,' Stella replied.

'Nor me.' Isabel was also refusing.

'I'd better go home,' Stefano said. 'We have a busy day ahead tomorrow.'

'Indeed yes. Thanks for the heads up on the workmen. We could have a difficult situation if they get their way.'

'I'm sure it can be avoided. I'll keep my ear to the ground and let you know if I find out anything. I'll say goodnight to you all. Thanks again for supper. As always, it was delicious.'

He walked to the door and Ignacio let him out. Stella felt strangely deprived as he left, which was quite ridiculous. She wondered what on earth had come over her. What was she expecting? Stefano to kiss her passionately before leaving?

She would see him again fairly soon, she had no doubt. Meanwhile, she had some work ahead to sort out her belongings. Thankfully, she hadn't brought a huge amount of clothes.

'I think I'll go up now, if you don't mind. I feel rather tired and it's been a busy day.'

'Of course, my dear,' Isabel said. 'See you in the morning. Do you think you might drive the boys on your own?'

'I think so. They know the way, don't they?'

'They do but don't trust them. They'll send you miles out of the way, given half a chance.' She laughed and said goodnight.

Stella went up to her room and stood looking at the heaps of clothes. What a stupid trick to play. She really couldn't imagine what had been behind the girl's thinking. Stella took out several coat hangers and began to hang her dresses on them to put in the wardrobe.

Really, she should have told Isabel, she was thinking. Perhaps tomorrow she might. With a sigh, she got ready for bed.

★　★　★

The week passed gently with a routine that had become fixed. She took the boys to school each day and found her way there easily, despite them giving her wrong directions each morning.

'There's a quick way if you turn right at the next roundabout,' Juan said cheerily.

'That would take us right into the sea, thank you very much.'

'We don't mind. We can take our shoes off and paddle.'

'You are going to school the way your mum uses.'

'Ah, well, I suppose we'll just have to spend the day being bored by our teachers.'

Stella smiled quietly to herself.

One day Isabel asked if she would

like to drive the two of them to the next town and do some shopping.

'There's a nice little boutique there and I want to look at some new dresses. Not that I really need any more but it's always good to look.'

'That sounds lovely. I could do with some more clothes myself. I don't have many things with me.'

'Do you want to send for some more? We can pay the postage if that's a problem.'

'Not really. I got rid of most of my old things. There are just a couple of sweaters and other oddments. I wasn't sure how much I'd need.'

'I hope you're not thinking of going back.'

'Oh, my goodness, no. As long as you are happy with me and what I'm doing.'

'My dear, you are already a big part of the family. We couldn't be more pleased with you.' Stella blushed again and murmured her thanks.

'In fact, I'd like to buy you something nice. Come on, let's go. It'll be fun. I'll tell Maria we're going out and won't need any lunch.'

Stella ran up to her room and collected her bag. She wondered about finding some way of locking her wardrobe but there was nothing she could use. She left it all with a sigh, hoping it would all still be in place on her return. But she expected it to be fine. After all, only Maria would be left in the house.

The two of them drove to the next town. Well, they called it the next town but it was quite a distance away.

'You really seem to be driving very well. Congratulations. You've taken to our weird Spanish roads. Now, if you go down the next turning on the left, there is some parking. The shops I want are very close by.'

Once they had parked, Stella took the wheelchair out of the boot and pushed it round to the side so Isabel could manoeuvre herself into it. She was amazed at the way she did it.

'Goodness me, you're good,' she told her.

'Practice, my dear. I can't be doing with messing around. I'd be grateful if you could push me, however. I'm not very good at wheeling myself.'

'No problems. I'm used to pushing my mum around. I'll just lock the car and we'll go.'

They spent a happy couple of hours looking at dresses and Stella tried some of them on. Once she had worked out the European sizes, she found several she liked. Now she actually had some money of her own, she could afford to buy one. But Isabel insisted on paying for it by the time she got to the checkout.

'But you can't. I mean it's very generous, but why should you?'

'I'd like to. No arguments. I said I would like to buy something for you and this is what I'm doing.'

'Goodness me, thank you so much.' Stella felt a bit awkward about accepting it but the woman was insisting. She hadn't even found anything she liked for herself, so it made it even worse.

The assistant was jabbering away in Spanish and Isabel answered her, obviously in what sounded very fluent Spanish.

Stella had no idea what was being said and stood awkwardly smiling. Her dress was wrapped and handed over after Isabel had paid with a card.

'There's another shop I'd like to visit. Do you mind pushing me along there?'

'Course not. Which way is it?'

'It's a bit of a way. Do you want to put your parcel in the car? Leave me here and do it. No need to carry it with us.'

Stella left her outside the shop and put her parcel in the car. She turned back and saw someone talking to Isabel. Hesitantly, she walked back, not wanting to get caught in another flow of Spanish that she couldn't understand. Isabel did not look happy. Her fists were clenched and she looked cross.

'Come on, Stella. Get me away from this man. He's rude and threatening.' The man was still speaking in Spanish and sounded angry. She told him to go away, or at least that's what Stella thought she was saying. She got behind the wheelchair and pushed her swiftly away.

'What was all that about?' she asked.

'Someone who used to work for Ignacio. He knew me from when I went to one of the company parties. Dreadful man. Ignacio sacked him a few weeks ago and he seemed to think I could persuade my husband to take him back. Makes me so mad. They seem to think it's all down to me.'

Stella went to look at her watch but she must have left it at home.

'Would you like to go for a coffee or something?'

'That would be nice. There's a bar along this road a bit further along.'

It was a pleasant bar, with several tables filled with women at this time of day. They sat down and soon a waiter came over. He bowed slightly and spoke in perfect English.

'What can I get for you?'

'How did you know we were English?' Stella asked in amazement.

'It's a knack I have. I am half English.'

'Goodness me, it seems most of the population of Spain is half English.'

'Besides, I know Señora Mendoza.' He smiled at her and she smiled back.

'I'll have a cappuccino, please.'

'I'd like the same,' Stella agreed.

'Two cappuccinos on their way. Anything to eat? I've got some excellent pastries.'

'Oh, go on, then. We'll both have one, thank you. You would like one, wouldn't you?' she asked her companion.

'Never say no to a pastry.'

'So tell me, how are you getting on with our Stefano?' Isabel asked. 'If you don't mind my asking, of course.'

'Very well. He's charming and of course, very good-looking.'

'It was nice he took you to meet his mother and sister. What did you make of her? Well of both of them, really.'

'I haven't had much experience of

anyone with Noelia's condition but she seemed a happy soul and seemed pleased to meet me. His mum is lovely. Joanne. A very English name.'

'His father left them a long time ago.'

'Left them? You mean he died?'

'No. He walked out on them after Stefano was born.'

'I didn't realise that. I suppose I assumed he had died. Poor woman. She must have found life very difficult with two little ones, especially one with special needs.'

'Stefano's been wonderful with both of them. He really cares for them.'

'Was that why you asked if I knew about his family life?'

'Well, yes. I didn't want you to fall for him and then discover he had people relying on him.'

'Fall for him?'

'Fall in love with him. I'm sorry but I saw the way you were looking at him right from the start.'

'I was looking at him? What do you mean?'

'Put it down to my ability to notice things. Admit it, you were . . . are . . . falling for him.'

Stella's cheeks burned.

'I . . . I don't know what to say. I suppose you're right. I am falling in love with him. Perhaps it's just the idea that he's different. That I'm in a strange place and receptive to his attentions.'

'Take care, love, that's all I'll say. Good, here comes the coffee.'

Stella was rather quiet for the rest of the time they were in the bar. Her thoughts were whizzing round and she felt slightly embarrassed that she had been so obvious. She plucked up courage to ask a question.

'Does Ignacio know how I feel? I mean — has he noticed anything.'

'Of course not. I doubt Stefano has noticed anything, either. It's a girl thing. Not that I'm a girl, of course. Perhaps I should say it's a female thing. So, how is he when you're alone?' she asked with a grin on her face.

'He's lovely.'

Stella blushed again. Perhaps she had been a bit forward with him and remembered how early in their relationship it was that they had kissed. She had assumed it was because of his half Spanish background. Besides which, she had never been sure how long she would be there for. She looked down, wondering how she might phrase it.

But Isabel spoke again.

'In your shoes I'd certainly have been interested in kissing Stefano. He is good-looking and he is charming. I really don't think you're making any mistakes.'

'You won't tell Ignacio, will you?'

'Course not. This between us. A secret, until you're ready to tell the world. Or even just Ignacio.'

They ate the light, crispy pastries and drank their coffee. It was all delicious. When they had finished, they went along to the next shop. This one had more young clothes and Stella fell in love with a top and trousers.

'I think I might treat myself to these. Does that seem greedy after your kindness?'

'Don't be silly. I'm going to buy myself a couple of tops as well. They are really gorgeous.'

'Do you want to try them?'

'I really can't be bothered. They are in my size so I'll risk it.'

'I'll use my new card to pay. Can you help me if I need it?'

'No problem. They speak English here so I don't think you'll have any difficulty.'

Fifteen minutes later, they emerged from the shop, both clutching bags with their new things inside. Stella felt very pleased with herself for managing and excited with her new things.

She would wear them when she next went out with Stefano . . . whenever that might be. They decided to eat at a bar in their own town and she drove back.

'Where shall we eat?' she asked.

'Go down to the playa and we'll stop

there somewhere. What about that place?'

'I don't know anywhere so wherever you'd like to go.'

They went inside and found a table with a sea view and a space for the wheelchair.

'Señora Mendoza. Is great to see you. How is your husband?'

'He's fine, thank you.'

'And your beautiful self? How are you?'

'I'm fine, too. This is a friend of ours. Stella, meet Diego.'

'How do you do?'

'Very well. I get you a menu and something to start. Will you have wine?'

'Sparkling water for me, please,' Stella said.

'Me, too. Thanks.' Isabel nodded. He bustled away to fetch their drinks. 'Sorry, I forgot this was his place. Hope you don't mind.'

'Course not. I think you're known everywhere. Disadvantage of being Ignacio's wife. Or perhaps it's an advantage.'

'Never really thought about it. I certainly felt it was a disadvantage when that chap spoke to me this morning. Awful man.'

'I agree. He should have shown respect to you, especially as you . . .' She stopped mid-sentence. She had been going to say as she was in a wheelchair.

'Especially as I'm in a wheelchair? Mind you, I do think I'm getting a bit stronger. I almost stood up on my own this morning. But, don't worry. I'm not sensitive to comments like that. It's a matter of fact, isn't it? No point trying to hide it.'

'I suppose not.' Stella felt marginally subdued and a great sense of admiration for this brave lady. What did she mean about feeling stronger lately?

After their lunch, they went home and Isabel went for a rest. She was quite exhausted after such a busy morning. Stella had an hour before she needed to leave to fetch the boys. She went to her room and lay on the bed.

She dozed slightly, thinking about the events that had happened to her since her arrival in Spain. Most of all she thought about Stefano and Isabel's words that morning.

Unfortunately, it was all a bit late. She knew inside that she had fallen for him, despite his family problems and the differences in their culture.

She gave a start, picked up her watch and realised it was way past the time she needed to leave for the boys. She would need to drive a little faster to get there in time. It was almost a quarter of an hour past their time when she arrived at the school.

Panting slightly, she almost ran towards the school from where she had parked. There were lots of parents standing around and all were waiting for their children to come out. She looked at her watch again and it still showed at least quarter of an hour past her usual time. Strange. At last the boys came out and ran towards her.

'Hi, there. Good day?'

'Excellent,' Javier said.

'Terrible,' Juan said. 'He doesn't know what he's in for when he moves up.'

'You seem to be late coming out. Were you kept in for some reason.'

'No. It's the usual time. Your watch must be fast.' Juan peered at his own watch and told her the right time.

Darn it, she was thinking. Maria must have altered it to make her worried about fetching the boys. Surely not, she told herself. That would be so childish. Perhaps she had done it herself when she took it off last night. Very strange.

'Have you got any biscuits for us today?' Javier asked hopefully. 'We like those chocolate ones you got once before.'

'Sorry. I thought I was late so no, I haven't got any. Perhaps Maria will have made something nice for you.'

'Maria's gone peculiar lately. She doesn't make anything nice for us.' He sounded so woebegone that Stella wanted to laugh but didn't dare as he'd probably be hurt.

'So, why did you have a terrible day?' she asked.

'Everything went wrong. I took the wrong book into Spanish and then couldn't do the math. It was awful.'

'Perhaps we can look at your maths when we get home. I'm not very good but maybe we can work on it together.'

'Thanks. That would be good. I could do with my dad's help with some things.'

'Perhaps he'll help you after dinner.'

But Ignacio didn't come home till way after they were in bed. Stella saw his face looking almost grey and realised something had gone badly wrong. She excused herself, assuming he'd want to talk it through with Isabel. She heard them both go to bed a short while later. He had looked very weary and careworn. She hoped it wasn't anything too serious. After all, that might affect Stefano, too.

Shock Accusations

Ignacio had already left before the boys had their breakfast. Stella hoped Juan would be in a happier mood this morning and he did seem to be.

'Where's Daddy?' Javier asked. 'We didn't even see him last night.'

'He was very late coming home. Now, have you finished eating? Go and clean your teeth and we'll go to school.'

'We need to see Mummy first.' They both left the table and rushed along to their parents' room. She heard them all chatting and sounding fairly happy. It was a relief.

Stella was feeling very concerned for both Isabel and Ignacio. She hoped it was nothing to do with their relationship and that it really was work connected. Maria came into the dining-room.

'You done with breakfast?'

154

'Yes, thank you.'

'Where boys are?'

'They're saying good morning to their mother. I shall be taking them to school soon.'

'Mother not well. I take breakfast to her when you have gone away.'

'I haven't spoken to her today.'

'Master, he tell me.'

'I'm sure you'll look after her very well.'

'Course I do. No lazy lazy woman like you.'

Stella refused to respond. She was by now, used to the epithet. She went to call the boys.

'Come on or you'll be late.' The pair of them scuttled out and went to their own bathrooms to clean their teeth.

'Come in,' Isabel called. Shyly, Stella went along to their room and tapped at the door.

'I'm sorry you're not well. Is there anything I can get for you?'

'I'm fine. Just a bit weary. We stayed awake chatting for too long last night.

I'll tell you about it later. That is if you don't mind, of course.'

'Not at all. I'd better go and collect those two and take them off. Thank you for trusting me,' she added as she left.

Stella's mind was very active as she drove back home again. What could be wrong? It must be to do with Ignacio's company. He couldn't possibly be having an affair or anything like that.

He adored his boys and she felt he wouldn't do anything to spoil his family life. He also seemed to adore Isabel. No, it must be something to do with his work. She hoped her friend would be up when she got back.

All seemed quiet when she arrived back at the house. She went to her room to tidy her bed then went down to the lounge. She heard Isabel moving around and waited for her. The door opened and she came in with her electric wheelchair.

'I heard you come in. Would you like a coffee? I certainly would. I'll call

Maria and she will bring us one.' Isabel said.

'Are you all right? I mean I was worried when Maria said you weren't well.'

'I was just tired. I'm quite well, thank you. I didn't sleep much last night by the time Ignacio had finished his tale of woe. Anyway, I'll ask Maria for coffee.' She went through to the kitchen.

Stella waited anxiously, wondering what on earth had been said by Ignacio last night. Isabel came back and settled down near Stella's chair.

'I'll wait till Maria's been in. Is all well with you?'

'Yes, thanks.' She paused, wondering whether to mention her watch being altered and of course, her clothes being taken out of the her wardrobe on Sunday. She decided not to give Isabel any more worries. Maria brought a tray of coffee in and put it down on the table near Stella.

'You pour it for boss lady.'

'Of course,' she replied, smiling

sweetly at the housekeeper. 'Not a problem.'

When they were both drinking their coffee and eating the cookies provided alongside, Isabel began to speak. Stella had already told her not to say anything she wasn't happy to confide with her.

'Ignacio's company is in trouble. Serious trouble. Someone has leaked a series of very special plans for a new product. It was almost ready to go public and they had hoped for massive orders from the government as well as private companies across Spain.

'Whoever has spilled the beans has ruined the chances of orders which may well go to another company.

'Unfortunately, one of their competitors has now got the plans and also the prototypes. Ignacio says they could go bust. They had put all their resources into this new project and the old ones had more or less been left to one side. It could be serious. It will mean a huge change to our lives.'

'Oh, goodness, I'm so sorry. That's

terrible. Have they any idea who is the guilty party?' Isabel looked away. She was having great difficulty in her next words.

'It looks like . . . it seems . . . it could be Stefano.' Stella went white. Not her lovely Stefano? Surely not him?

'Our Stefano.' She nodded unhappily.

'It looks like it.'

'But how do you know? I mean what's he done to . . . to make himself an . . . object of suspicion?' She was tumbling over the words and hating what she was hearing.

'I'm not sure but it seems he was pretty much the only one with computer access to all the plans. I don't know if they had anyone else who worked with him.'

'But it seems so unlike him.'

'Money can be a big incentive. We don't know how much he needed at home. Perhaps someone needs an operation or extra help. He would have been paid a vast amount for this — assuming it was him, of course.'

'Goodness. I find it almost impossible to believe.' She went quiet for a while. 'I suppose it will be the end of my time here. And Maria, too. How will you manage?'

'It's still early days. We will have to sell this place, of course, and as the market is falling, we won't get a huge amount for it. It's all such a mess. I'm sorry to pour it all out to you but I see you as a friend. A sort of companion.'

'Well, thank you. I promise you I won't breathe a word of it to anyone else. Not that I know anyone else. But obviously the boys will have to be kept in the dark for now. Oh goodness, what about their school? That must cost you a fortune.'

'It certainly does, especially now there are two of them going there. The uniform alone costs a fortune. Sorry, my mind is running free with it all.'

'Where is Stefano now?'

'I'm not sure. I think he's still working there but Ignacio said the police will be called in later this morning. I suppose he could even be under arrest eventually.

'I know you are very fond of him but he may be guilty. I know you won't want to believe that but it has to be faced.'

'If I'm going back to the UK, it probably won't make any difference to me, will it?' Stella got up. Just when everything was going so well, all this had to happen. Hadn't she already suffered her fair share of things going wrong? What would she do when she got back to England? She'd have nowhere to live and no job.

She flopped down on her bed, tears streaming from her eyes. She thought of Stefano . . . his lovely face, his dark hair and brown eyes. Beautiful brown eyes. And when he kissed her, he was . . . wonderful. How could someone like that be guilty of such awful things?

After some while, she had no idea how long it had been, she heard Isabel coming upstairs in the lift. She tapped on Stella's door.

'Can I come in?' she asked.

'Of course. I'm sorry. I just didn't want to believe any of it.'

'Nor me, love. I didn't want to believe it, either. We just have to wait and see. Now, come down and have some lunch. Maria's put out some cold meat and salad.'

'I couldn't eat a thing.'

'You must try. Come on. There might be nothing in the cupboard tomorrow. You'll be glad of bread and scrape.'

'Goodness, I haven't heard that for many years. My granny used to say that when I was little.' She smiled and went down with Isabel in the lift.

'Remember, say nothing in front of Maria, nor the boys,' Isabel urged. 'We don't want anything getting out. Not yet.'

'Of course not. Nor, I presume do I let on that I know to Ignacio.'

'I'll tell him later I've confided in you. Now. Come and eat something.'

All went as normal for the rest of the day. Stella fetched the boys home and spent time with them doing their homework. After this, they went to play on their computer and she sat with them and pretended to know about Minecraft.

They showed her round their latest creation and she pretended to be impressed. Then it was almost dinner time and she sent them to wash their hands. Stella and Isabel were both very surprised when Ignacio came home with Stefano.

'Hope we can stretch the meal for him as well,' Ignacio said. He looked very tired and strained.

Maria was muttering away but there was plenty of food for everyone. Stella found it very difficult to be natural with Stefano, claiming eventually that she had a headache. When they all had eaten, Isabel told the boys it was time for bed.

'Oh,' Juan moaned, 'we wanted to play a game.'

'Not tonight. Come on, be good.'

Ignacio promised to read them a

story as long as they went off quickly. They went off grumbling but soon they were in their beds with a pile of books ready for their father. Isabel was wonderful, Stella thought. She chatted about their day and told Stefano about their trip into town the previous day.

'It was all fun, wasn't it, Stella?'

'It was. Isabel bought me a lovely dress and then I bought some trousers and a top,' she said feebly. Her mind was racing round and she was wondering why Ignacio had brought Stefano home if he was guilty of well . . . ruining his business.

'Would you mind if we took a walk round the garden, Isabel?'

'Please, carry on. Ignacio will be back soon.'

They went outside into the cool air and walked down to the bottom of the garden. The orange blossom smelled wonderful and everything seemed almost ghostly quiet.

'I assume you know the problems we have. It was pretty obvious during the meal that you knew.'

'Isabel did confide in me today. I don't think she's told Ignacio that she did but perhaps she's telling him now. Why did you do it?'

'I have done nothing. I promise you. The police think it was me because of my expertise with the computers. But I'm certainly not the only one in the company who can press a few keys.'

'Have you been arrested?'

'Of course not. I have spent the day at the Guardia Civil being questioned but they can't pin anything on me. I must say, it was all horrible. They want to question me again tomorrow so I'm facing another long day. Do you believe me?'

'I don't really know much about it. I suppose I want to, very much. It's difficult to think you could have done such a deed to someone like Ignacio who has treated you so well.' She felt tears pressing behind her eyes and felt glad it was dark outside and he couldn't see them.

'Please Stella, you must believe me.'
He put his arm round her shoulders
and tried to turn her towards him. She
resisted and hated herself for not
responding. Somehow, she felt it was
wrong.

'I'm sorry, Stefano. I need time to
absorb what you're saying. It was such a
shock when Isabel told me and I didn't
want to believe it at all. I want you to be
innocent.'

'I see. It's not enough that Ignacio
believes me.'

'I'm sorry but I'm still feeling so
confused. Give me time to think. It was
all a bit of a shock. Let's go back inside.
Ignacio should have finished his bedtime story.'

They went back and after about half
an hour's difficult chat, Stefano rose
and said his goodnights.

'Don't worry, Stefi, it'll all sort out in
the end. Tomorrow may be difficult for
all of us but hopefully, after that, all will
be well. Mark my words. We shall find
the guilty culprit,' Ignacio said.

'Thanks for having faith in me. Thanks to you, Isabel, for dinner. Goodnight.'

Stella muttered goodnight as he left.

'You must believe him,' Ignacio told her. 'I cannot believe he did those terrible things. The police will sort it out and meantime, I'm looking at everyone who worked on the project. Now, I'm going to bed. I'm exhausted.'

The two women sat quietly for a few moments.

'I don't really know who to believe,' Stella said eventually. 'I presume you told Ignacio that you had confided in me.'

'I did. He didn't mind. He realised I needed someone to speak to and you were the obvious choice.'

'Well, thank you. What do you think?'

'Ignacio doesn't believe it was Stefano so that's good enough for me. I hope you can think that way too. Even if not now, eventually.'

'I hope so. I think I feel confused about my feeling for Stefano and all of this. I really think I've fallen in love with him but it scares me.'

'Let's wait and see what happens tomorrow. Now, I think it's time for bed. Goodnight and do try to sleep.'

'I will. Goodnight.'

Stella went up to her room and lay on the bed. Sleep was a long way off and she turned everything over and over in her mind.

A Woman's Work . . .

When her alarm went off the next morning, Stella came to with a start. She was still dressed from the previous day and was lying on top of the bed. Quickly, she peeled off her clothes and dashed under the shower. She dressed again and went to the boys' rooms.

'Time to get up,' she told them. 'Come on now, we don't want to be late. I think it's your sporty day today, isn't it?' One day a week the whole school went dressed in their sporty clothes. Evidently it saved them having to change when they did their activities.

'I hate sports,' Juan announced.

'I love sports,' Javier contradicted. 'It's good fun.'

'You just wait till you're in my year. You won't love it then.'

They continued bickering while they

dressed and eventually arrived down-stairs ready for breakfast.

'Where's breakfast?' Juan demanded. 'Maria hasn't made it ready for us.'

'I don't know. Perhaps I'll find Maria and see.' She knew she wasn't going to get any sympathy from the housekeeper as she knocked at the door. She opened it cautiously and looked into the kitchen.

There was nobody there and all the previous night's dishes were piled around the room. She wondered what she should do and decided to look for cereal and fruit. There was a dish of fruit on the side and cereal in one of cupboards. She piled things on to a tray and took them through.

'Maria isn't there,' she told the two boys. 'I'll go and find some milk and you can eat some fruit in the meantime.'

She went back into the kitchen and looked in the fridge. Milk was there and also fruit juice. She poured milk into a jug and took the carton of juice as it was. The boys laughed and poured out large glasses.

'We should always have juice poured like that. Much more sensible than dirtying a jug.' Juan was quite advanced in his years, Stella was thinking.

'I wonder what's happened to Maria,' she said to no-one in particular.

'Perhaps she doesn't like washing up any more. Or cooking.'

'Maybe. I suppose I'd better do it when I get back from school, if Maria hasn't turned up.'

'There's a dishwasher. You won't have to do it.'

'No, but I shall have to load it. And clear up the remains of last night's meal. Come on, finish your cereal and let's get ready for school. You can have a muesli bar if you're still hungry.' Stella had noticed them in a jar in the kitchen and went to fetch one each for the boys.

At last they were ready and set off for school. The mystery of Maria's absence would have to wait for a while, at least till Stella got back.

Did Isabel know about it, and what of Ignacio? Her mind raced round all the new complications of her life. She could well be heading back to England fairly soon anyway so perhaps her worries were all pointless.

She drove back to the house and let herself in. Everything was quiet and it seemed no-one was there. She went to Isabel's room and knocked on her door.

'Come in,' Isabel called. 'Sorry, I'm still in bed. Couldn't face getting up.'

'Are you unwell?' Stella asked.

'Not really. I just feel depressed. I rang the bell for Maria to bring me some coffee but for some reason, she didn't answer.'

'Yes, well, Maria's disappeared. Last night's supper things are still around the kitchen and she's gone. Or maybe she's just gone for the morning.'

'Really? I can't think why. Nor where she's gone to. This is her home. Have you been to look into her room?'

'Of course not. I didn't want my

head blown off. In fact, I'm not even sure which is her room.'

'It's beyond the kitchen. Haven't you noticed the door at the rear of the room? That leads through to her quarters. Perhaps you should look in there. See if she's not well or something.'

Stella nodded and feeling somewhat apprehensive of the bad-tempered woman, went through the kitchen and knocked at the door Isabel had mentioned. There was no reply. She opened it and called out Maria's name. Silence.

She went along to another door and knocked at that but there was still no response. Taking a deep breath, she opened it, to find the room was empty. The bed in the corner was unmade and she looked in the wardrobe and saw that was empty. Maria had obviously left the house. Why, she could only guess. She went back to Isabel's room and told her the news.

'She's obviously got wind of the

problems though exactly how, I don't know.'

'Could she have heard you talking about to me yesterday morning?'

'Unlikely, I'd have thought, but perhaps she did. She may have waited behind the door. And perhaps heard more last night.'

'Where do you think she's gone?'

'Possibly to stay with her sister. Mother of the girl she wanted us to employ to do your job.'

'I'd better go and clear up the kitchen.'

'I'm sorry. Do you mind?'

'Course not. I'll make some coffee too and bring some for you.'

Stella went into the kitchen and began to tackle the mountain of pans and crockery, then she wiped over the surfaces. It looked much better but it had taken her a long time.

She looked for the coffee machine and saw it was still full of grounds and some coffee was left in the jug. With a sigh she emptied it and put clean water and more fresh grounds in and switched it on.

Stella looked for a toaster and found one in a cupboard. She popped a couple of slices of bread into it and watched to make sure it worked. She put things on to a tray, expecting to take it for Isabel. The door opened and she came into the room.

'Wow, that's terrific. Well done you. I'm so sorry you had to do it.'

'Not a problem. I've made toast and coffee for you. Where do you want it?'

'Let's sit in here. Take advantage of being able to use our own kitchen.'

They sat round the table enjoying a new experience. Isabel told Stella about Maria's introduction to the house. She had taken over the kitchen and all that was associated with ordering food and preparing meals.

'I don't even know how much she was spending each week. Pathetic, aren't I? Ignacio paid the bills and I just left it to them. I suppose I should get involved to a much greater degree now.

Goodness knows who will do the cooking.'

'I can do simple stuff but mostly English cooking. I'm not sure I could manage the sort of things Maria makes.'

'I couldn't impose on you. It's far too much for you to do.'

'I'm not taking it on as a permanent thing. I can help out for a while, providing you don't mind English-style food. Sausage and mash and maybe steak pies occasionally. Nothing very special.'

'That sounds amazing. You know, I'd forgotten about good old English food. See what's in the freezers first and we can decide what to do about ordering what you need. I can peel vegetables and chop things sitting here. It could be fun.'

'I'm not sure what Ignacio will make of it.'

'Don't worry about him. He's so busy organising stuff and coming to terms with what has happened. We have far bigger things to worry about. Perhaps I might call Ignacio and see what he's doing. See what he's found out, if anything. It's all so very worrying.'

Stella could see she was nearly in tears and wondered what she could say to make things better but there was really nothing. She went to look in the freezer to see what she might cook that evening. She opened the door and saw nothing but empty shelves. She went to the second freezer and in that one were a few vegetables and that was all. The fridge told the same story. Apart from half a dozen eggs and a piece of cheese, there was almost nothing. No more bread and only a couple of jars of jam.

Maria must have cleared out everything. It was all very strange, she was thinking. She went to see where Isabel was. How was she going to take this latest piece of news? Isabel was in the lounge, her hand over the phone.

'I couldn't decide whether to call or not. If he's in the middle of something, he wouldn't appreciate me calling. Oh dear, I don't know what to do.'

'I'm afraid I've got some bad news. The freezer is empty. No meat or fish and only a few vegetables in the other one. And there's virtually nothing left in the fridge.'

'What? That's ridiculous. That wretched woman must have cleared the lot. I know there was a lot of meat in there as we had a delivery recently. How on earth did she carry it away?'

'She must have had transport. Someone with a car or van? It must have been during the night. I didn't hear anything, did you? She must have called someone late last night and they came to fetch her.'

There were tears forming in Isabel's eyes. She looked almost desperate and Stella hated having to tell her this latest bit of news. She also felt like crying but managed to keep control of herself.

'I know there was plenty of food,' she wailed.

'Perhaps we — or I — should go to

the supermarket and get something for a day or two? Do you know where Maria's sister lives? Do you want to go round and tackle her?'

'There's no point. They'll stick together and claim they know nothing. Maria has always been a bit difficult but her sister is much worse than she is. I think we'll just have to accept it.'

'Perhaps deduct it from her pay?'

'It's almost the end of the month. She'll have been paid already. No, we just have to accept it as a loss. Perhaps a trip to the supermarket will be the answer. I'd better come with you as I have a card to pay with. We'll need to set the burglar alarm, too. I daren't leave the house unguarded. I'll tell Ignacio and we can go.'

Isabel phoned the office and asked to speak to her husband. He was not available, she was told. She asked for a message to be given to him and she was ready.

Stella drove to the Mercadona and helped Isabel out of the car and into

179

her wheelchair. They walked round the different aisles, seeming almost familiar to Stella, as it was similar to home. Isabel was fascinated as she rarely ever went into food shops.

'I can't believe the variety of things available. So much choice. Things I've never even heard of.' Stella laughed.

'We need to make our choices and go back home. We need bread and cold meats. At least that is slightly Spanish. Butter and cheese. Then we need to look at the meat counter. Or do you want fish? And some fresh vegetables and salad stuff.'

'Goodness. I think you should go and stock up with whatever you think. Leave me here for a bit.'

'Are you sure? You won't be too bored.'

'I can't cope with all the dashing around finding things. Go on, if you don't mind, of course.'

'I'll do my best.' Stella went off with the trolley and loaded all the things she thought they might need. It was difficult guessing what the family liked and didn't, though she had a pretty good idea after living with them for a while.

No way could she make the complicated desserts that Maria seemed to manage so she bought ready-made ones and hoped nobody would notice. The trolley was full as she made her way back to the checkout area where she had left Isabel.

'Goodness,' she said. 'Thank heavens you went on your own. I'd have been feeling quite dizzy finding all that lot. Let's go and pay.'

Stella unloaded the shopping and the girl put it through the checkout. Isabel took out her credit card and handed it to the girl. She spoke in Spanish and Stella listened in horror as she gathered the card was being refused.

'What's wrong?' she asked.

'Evidently this card has been cancelled. I have another we can try.' That one too was cancelled. 'My bank debit card should work,' she muttered. It also was cancelled. Isabel was almost in tears.

'I've got my card. Perhaps that one will work.'

'You can't pay for all this.'

'It's only temporary. Call it a loan.'

The queue behind them was getting angry. One woman was quite aggressive and began to spout a stream of words that fortunately, Stella didn't understand. She muttered that she was English and the woman stopped her curses. Her card was accepted and they went out with all their shopping. The car was almost full by the time it was all loaded and an angry Isabel was letting her feelings run riot.

'How could he allow us to get into this state? Why do they have to cancel our cards? How did it happen? I really don't understand it.'

They drove back to the house and went into the garage. Ignacio's car was parked there.

'Goodness, what's he doing home?' Isabel said.

'Let's get you in and we can unload the shopping later.'

Ignacio was in the kitchen with Stefano making coffee.

'Where's Maria?' was his first question.

'She's gone. Emptied our freezer and fridge and left. We've just been shopping and my cards don't work any more. Poor Stella had to pay with her card. We must reimburse her. It must have nearly emptied her account.' Then she burst into tears.

'All right, my love. It's all right. It will get sorted, I promise you. I have some money in another place. We won't be destitute.'

'Do you want some help with the shopping?' Stefano asked.

'Well, yes please. The car is pretty full.' Stella led the way down to the garage and they began to take the carrier bags out. 'Let's put them in the lift and then we don't have to carry them up. How are you, anyway?'

'Not brilliant. It seems they have

decided I'm not guilty of sending stuff away to competitors, which is a great relief.'

'Thank goodness for that. I was so worried. I didn't want to believe it but it did look pretty damning.'

'I didn't sleep last night at all. Pity I wasn't here. I might have heard Maria stealing all their food.' They both laughed slightly. 'It's good to see you smile again. Oh Stella, Stella, please say you didn't believe I was capable of such terrible damage to the company.'

'I'm sorry but I couldn't help it. It all seemed so definite and you were the one they blamed. But if they say it wasn't you, that's fine.' She put her hand on his arm and gave it a squeeze. He swung round and kissed her.

'Thank you for that, anyway. The only snag is, they now think Ignacio himself might be guilty.'

'What? No way.'

'Think about it. He had a process that was going to revolutionise his product and they think he sold it to his competitors for a huge sum of money. Enough to keep him going for many years. His company would close but he'd have plenty of money.'

'But surely not. You don't believe that he's capable of that, do you?'

'I didn't. But there are some facts that make it a bit of a mystery. Cancelling credit cards, for instance. That is typical of some sort of suspicion.'

'I wondered if they had been hacked. Could the company have been hacked?'

'I doubt it. Although I suppose it's possible. Nobody has suggested that.'

'Let's take this lot upstairs. There's stuff that needs to go in the freezer and other things need refrigerating.'

Having something positive to do made Stella feel better. Stefano's comments about Ignacio had upset her more than she realised. Surely he couldn't have damaged his own company? But he did mention that he had some other money. Did that signify anything? She unloaded some of the meat and stowed it in the freezer. The rest she put in the fridge ready for supper that night. She realised they would need something to eat now and set out some of the cooked meats she had bought and put salad in a bowl. There were also some rolls which she put out, all in the kitchen. Stefano watched her and smiled at her efficiency.

'Well done. I'll go and fetch the other two. Not sure where they went to but I'll find them.'

She glanced at the clock. It was only just over an hour before she needed to fetch the boys from school. Then there was the evening meal to sort out and homework to supervise. She was going to be busy for the rest of the day.

She had once wondered what Maria did with herself all day but she was beginning to realise there was more to keeping this house than she'd known. All very well for Stefano to smile as she laid out the food but he might have helped. Then she thought he wouldn't know much about helping in this house. He obviously did lots at his own home to help his mother and sister.

Nobody ate much in the circumstances and Stella put a lot of the food back in the fridge. They were discussing the next move as they ate. Ignacio spoke most of all.

'They seem to think it's all down to me. I'm lucky to be here with you all and not locked away somewhere. I have to meet with lawyers later today and then perhaps I shall have to go to the Guardia Civil headquarters. But please don't worry, Isabel. They don't have any reason to keep me there.'

'You say that. But how do I know you can mean it? They've frozen our accounts and we have no money. How can we manage?'

'I've told you. I have other money. I'll get some and give it to you.' He left the room and went into his study. He came back with a bundle of notes and handed them to his wife. 'See? That should last you for a while.'

'At least I can pay Stella back for our food. And what are we going to do about Maria?'

'Forget her. She thinks she's got away with her robbery and let her have it. We shall get even with her one day. If we can manage for a while, we can find a new cook soon.'

'Oh, Ignacio. You are so foolish. We can't carry on living here. The boys will have to leave their expensive school.'

'And I must go back to England,' Stella chipped in. 'I'd better go and collect the boys while I can.' She looked at the unhappy group and picked up the car keys.

'May I come with you?' Stefano asked.

'I . . . er . . . I don't know.'

'Please do. The boys will be thrilled,' Isabel said. 'You might enjoy having company too.' Stella gave a shrug and he followed her down to the garage.

'You don't mind, do you?'

'Of course not. In fact you can drive. Here.' She handed him the keys.

'If you like. Are you really sure you don't mind my coming with you? You do seem a bit off.'

'I don't know what to think any more. I suppose I'm just tired. It's all been quite a shock to the system and with Maria leaving us in the lurch, it's all down to me now.

'And as I said, I don't think I'm going to be able to stay here much longer. I've got nowhere to go to if I do return to England. Oh, I've got friends but I wouldn't want to impose on them.'

After that little outburst, they remained quiet for most of the journey. Near the school, he parked the car and they sat in it, waiting for it to be time the boys were released.

'Shall we go?' Stefano asked after a few minutes. 'I'll go if you want to stay here.'

'Of course not. I'll come, too.' He tried to take her hand as they walked to the school but she shook him away. He looked hurt but said nothing. When the boys came out, they flung themselves at the man.

'Why aren't you busy at work?' Juan asked.

'I've got the day off. Specially to come and help Stella with you two.'

'Why do you need to help her?'

'Cos I know you two. What say we stop and get an ice-cream?'

'Oh, yes. Can we, Stella?'

'Of course. Come on, then. Let's get back in the car.'

What Does the Future Hold?

'Are we going for pizzas tonight?' Javier asked.

'I don't think so. Why would we?'

'Cos it's Friday and we always go on Fridays.'

'No, it isn't. It's only Thursday,' Juan corrected him.

The two of them argued about what day it was as they reached the ice-cream shop. They immediately stopped and clambered out of the car and ran into the shop. Stefano shrugged and got out to follow them.

'I want passion fruit, please,' Juan said.

'And I want cherry, please,' Juan announced.

'What will you have?' Stefano asked Stella.

'Coffee,' the two boys said in unison.

'How do you know that?'

'Stella told us it was her favourite. She's bound to choose that.'

'Coffee, please,' she confirmed. They all laughed and she suddenly felt better.

It had been such a difficult day. They crossed the road to the seat where they'd sat before and all enjoyed their ice-creams.

'Thank you so much. I haven't got any money with me so I can't pay you back,' Stella said.

'Don't be silly. My treat.'

'But you . . . never mind. Thank you. Come on, then. Let's get you home and clean off the ice-cream debris.'

'Maria won't have to give us any biscuits or cakes or anything. We can say we've had ice-creams,' Javier said cheerfully.

'Maria isn't there,' Stella told them.

'See, I said it was Friday,' Javier announced.

'No, it isn't.' Juan was adamant.

'I'm going to cook dinner this

evening,' Stella said. 'You can help once you've finished your homework. I'm going to make something very English . . . something I used to make for my mum.'

'What will that be?'

'Steak and kidney pie.'

'Ugh, I hate kidney.'

'I'm sure you'll like my pie.'

'So where's Maria?'

'I'm not sure. She left in the night. But you remember she wasn't here when we had breakfast.'

'But you said she'd gone out or something.'

'Yes, well, I was mistaken. Come on, we're almost home. Get ready to see your parents. Daddy's home as well.'

'Yeah!' the two boys called out, dashing out of the car as soon as it was stopped.

'They are never going to understand what will happen to them. What do you think will happen to Ignacio? Might he go to prison?' Stella asked Stefano.

'Mightn't we both? I really don't

know. I only know we're both innocent but unless they can find out the guilty person and prove it, maybe we will both end up in prison.'

Stella sat silently for a moment, then she gave a big sigh and got out of the car. She hated the uncertainty and nobody knowing the truth. It was so unfair on the two little boys and Isabel, too, of course. She could never manage on her own.

But how could she afford to keep Stella here? She needed some pay, of course, but perhaps not as much as she was getting at the moment. She went into the lounge where the family were all sitting.

'Have you got some homework to do?' she asked the boys.

'Yes. Daddy says he'll help us tonight. I like having him at home, don't you, Juan?'

'Course I do. I don't know why he's home and why Stefano's here, but it's good.'

'You go and make a start. I'm sure

your dad will come and help when he's ready.' She looked at Ignacio and he nodded. He looked so pale and strained, she really felt for him. Isabel also look strained and almost ready to burst into tears.

'Do you want to go home, Stefano? You're welcome to stay if you want to but please do whatever suits you best.'

'If you don't mind, I'd like to stay. It's the thought of your steak and kidney pie, of course. Sounds wonderful.'

'I don't know if it will be. Everything's different here. I'll go and put the meat on to cook anyway.' Stella went into the kitchen, feeling almost nervous. It was so much Maria's territory that anything she touched, she felt guilty.

She found a pan and put the meat into it with water and seasoning. Onions were added and she put it on the stove to simmer. Then she went back into the lounge where she had left Isabel and Stefano. As she walked in, their conversation stopped suddenly.

'Sorry, am I interrupting something?'

'We were just saying how good it is to have you here. I don't know what we'd have done on our own.' Isabel was generous with her praise.

'Well, thank you. I haven't really done a lot.'

'You're here when needed,' Stefano said. 'And you have helped Isabel when she most needed help. Besides, you're a very nice person to have around.'

'I'm not sure about that. But again, thank you for saying it.'

It felt slightly strange to Stella. Her role had changed overnight. Instead of being the typical au pair, she now seemed to be in charge of the kitchen and the boys and also a counsellor of some sort.

She had no idea of what was going to happen long term and she hated that. If she was going to be needed to stay, what was her future to be?

She didn't mind not getting paid in the short term but long term, it was different. For the time being, though, she was happy to help out in whatever way she could.

She looked round the beautiful room and wondered how long it might be theirs. The whole house was wonderful, from the basement swimming pool to the top floor patio.

What on earth would the boys think if they had to move out of their home? How would they feel about moving away from their private school? She gave a shudder at the thought.

'Are you feeling cold?' Stefano asked, who had clearly been watching her.

'Not really. I was just thinking about the future. Wondering what it holds for us all.'

'I'm very concerned about what will happen to my mother and sister. I know the house is mine so presumably they can't seize that. I've put it in my mother's name anyway to make sure she always has a home.'

'That was kind of you.'

'Practical rather than kind. It was all down to a large bonus from Ignacio that enabled me to buy it in the first place. It's not a huge place but at least they are accommodated.'

'I'm glad about that, Stefano. I did wonder how you would spend that money but I should have known you'd do something like that.' Isabel smiled at him and took his hand and gave it a squeeze.

'I'd better go and make the pastry. I hope it's going to work. I can only just remember how to do it,' Stella said.

She went into the kitchen and began her work. The meat seemed to have cooked satisfactorily. She made the pastry the way she used to make it for her mum. It seemed to work reasonably well. She finished off the pie and put it in the oven. It seemed a bit lost in the huge space but she also put in some jacket potatoes, prepared some vegetables and left them ready to cook later.

She went through to lay the table. Back in the lounge, the boys had come down, having finished their homework.

Ignacio was also there, a glass held in his hand. The other two weren't drinking and Stella settled down.

'How did you get on?' Isabel asked.

'It's all cooking. Hope it will be OK. I haven't made a pudding but there are yogurts if anyone wants more.'

'It's good of you to help us like this,' Ignacio said. 'It won't be for long before we get another cook.'

'Oh, Ignacio, you can't say that. We simply don't know what the future holds for us.'

'Why not?' Juan asked. 'I don't know what you mean.'

Isabel bit her lip. She had forgotten the boys were in the room as she spoke.

'Daddy has a problem at work. We don't know what will happen yet.'

'What sort of a problem?' he asked.

'It's all a bit complicated. Nothing to worry you with. Anyone else want a drink?' Ignacio asked, pouring himself another large brandy.

'Be careful, darling. Don't have too much.'

'Heavens, Isabel. I'm not drinking too much. You don't seem to realise the problems I'm facing. For goodness' sake, you don't understand what I'm going through. I could be arrested at any moment. That would mean goodbye to all of this.' He swept his arms round the room and swallowed his brandy.

Javier burst into tears and Juan went over to him and put his arms round him. He, too, was almost in tears.

'It's all right, Javier, don't worry. I'll look after you, like I do at school sometimes,' Juan assured him.

'But you can't look after me like Daddy and Mummy do. What does he mean he might be arrested?'

'I'm sorry, boys. I didn't mean to scare you. My company is having some problems and the Guardia Civil are asking me lots of questions about it.'

'Did you do it?' Juan asked.

'Course I didn't. I'd never do anything like that. Why would I jeopardise my own company? Someone has found out about one of our processes and copied all the files and sent them to one of our competitors. We have to find out who it was.'

'Could it have been Stefano?'

'Of course not.'

'Well, he does most of your computer stuff, doesn't he?'

'I do,' Stefano said stiffly. 'But I'd never do anything like that. Why would I do it? Any more than Ignacio would do it.'

'OK,' Juan replied chirpily. 'Just thought it for a minute. Will you help me with Minecraft?'

'I think we're going to have supper in a few minutes. I think you'll have to manage Minecraft on your own for now.'

'I'll go and put the vegetables on. Then we can eat. Oh, I've just remembered, I also bought something we can have for pudding,' Stella told them. Javier laughed.

'We don't have puddings. We have dessert.'

'My mistake.' Stella smiled.

Her pie turned out beautifully. Everyone was most enthusiastic and second helpings were asked for. She felt very relieved.

Ignacio had produced a bottle of wine to go with the meal and was by now, getting quite merry. Isabel was faintly apologetic about his state. Stella cleared the empty dishes away and put them all in the dishwasher. Stefano came into the kitchen with a collection of things.

'Well done, Stella. That was a terrific meal.'

'Thank you. Think I may have got myself another job as cook.'

'Don't let yourself get put upon.'

'I won't, but there is only me to help out. Isabel can't do it and Ignacio isn't likely to even try. Someone has to look after them all. I don't mind for the time being. They are extraordinary circumstances.'

'You're right, of course. I was rather hoping . . . well, that there might be a future for us. What do you think.'

'Oh, Stefano . . . I honestly don't know. I did think there could be but that was before all this stuff with Ignacio's company.

'I just feel the uncertainty makes me a bit negative about Spain and my own future. I'm sorry. Give me a little time to know what's going to happen and then I'll think.'

'Very well. But you do care, don't you?'

'Of course I do. But if I have to go back to England, what's the point?'

'But I'd look after you.'

'Exactly how would you do that if you're out of work? You don't know that you're clear yet anyway. Not with the police. Now, I'd better get the pudding out.'

'We don't have puddings here. They are desserts.' He spoke and then grinned. Stella couldn't help but smile.

'Go on with you. See if there's anything else that needs to go in the dishwasher.'

The meal was finished and Stella and Stefano played a card game with the two boys. Then it was bedtime and Stella took them upstairs and read them a story.

* * *

Ignacio was slumped in an armchair looking very miserable and, as she thought, slightly drunk. The boys were very excited and she had a job to quieten them down. At last they did seem to settle and she went down to the lounge room again. She heard raised voices as she arrived there.

'But Ignacio, even if you're innocent, the company might still go into liquidation. You heard what they said.

'If that happens we shall have to move and sell this place. Our whole lives will change. What shall I do without someone to cook the food for us all? And the boys will have to change their school, as we've said so many times.'

'I do not know,' Ignacio replied,

exasperated. He then went into Spanish and Stella did not understand a word of what she was hearing. Stefano joined in and she felt totally left out of the conversation or rather, row that had broken out. Isabel noticed she had come back into the room and spoke in English again.

'Please excuse us,' she said to Stella. 'We were discussing our next move.'

'Which will be nowhere.' Ignacio was furious and didn't want to say anything else. He got up from his chair and disappeared into his office.

'Leave him,' Isabel said. 'He needs time on his own.'

Once Ignacio had left them, the atmosphere changed into something a little more social. Isabel chatted as if she were hosting the evening and spoke as if nothing serious had happened. At last Stefano rose, and said that he ought to go home.

'But where's your car?' Stella asked.

'Still at work. I can walk home. It's not far.'

'Stella can drive you back, can't you?'

'Well, yes, of course. As long as you don't mind.'

'Thanks, that's kind.'

They went down to the garage and got into Isabel's small car. They drove round to his house quickly and as she stopped he reached over to her and kissed her.

'Something for you to remember me by. I hope you'll give some thought to our future.'

'Like I said, I need more time.' Inside she knew she wanted to stay and be with him but it was all too difficult at the moment. 'Night, Stefano. Sleep well, or at least try to.' She drove away and was soon back at home. She knew all about roundabouts now and would never go the wrong way again.

Isabel was ready to go to bed when she returned home.

'I don't know what Ignacio is doing but I'm going to bed now,' she told Stella. 'Will you go up soon? You must be exhausted after the traumas of today.'

'I'll empty the dishwasher first. And possibly lay breakfast. Save time in the morning.'

'I'm so sorry you're having to do it.'

'No worries. I really don't mind.'

Isabel thanked her and disappeared through the door into her bedroom. Stella went into the kitchen and began to empty the machine. She put things away to a certain extent but left out things for breakfast.

Suddenly, she felt very weary and decided to leave the table till tomorrow. At least she would be prepared for it the next day rather than this morning when Maria's departure had come as such a shock. What would tomorrow bring, she wondered.

Strangely, she fell asleep the moment her head touched the pillow. She had expected to lie awake thinking, as she had the previous night.

She woke up with a start and leapt out of bed. She must have forgotten to set the alarm and was already late. Perhaps she had better miss her shower and get ready right away. She called the boys and they were already up and bouncing around.

'Come on, you two. Get dressed and come down quickly. We're late. I'll go and get breakfast ready.'

She ran down the stairs to the kitchen. She put out cups and bowls and various things for them to eat and drink. She made toast and soon, it was all ready for them. They would enjoy the novelty of eating in the kitchen.

'Wow, this is fun. We only ever have snacks in here after school.'

As soon as they had finished, Stella sent them to clean their teeth and say goodbye to their parents. As it turned out, it was just their mother. Ignacio had already left for work.

She drove them to school and then went back home to see Isabel. They needed to discuss the day and also to plan the meals. She also needed to do some washing for the boys and herself. It looked like being a busy day. She knocked at the door of her employer.

'Can I bring you some coffee?' she asked.

'I'm getting up. Come in please, dear. I've got slightly stuck.' Isabel was sitting right at the edge of her bed struggling with a pair of trousers. 'I got halfway into them and seem to have got both legs in into one leg, if you know what I mean.'

'I'll help you. Here, let me pull them off you and start again.' Soon she was dressed and sitting in her electric wheelchair.

'Thank you so much. Ignacio usually helps me but he's already gone. I've been thinking, I really need to go the physiotherapist to get some help.

'I'm sure I've improved in my upper body strength and I'd like to try walking with a frame again. I used to be able to but then I gave up and sank into this chair. Would you be willing to take me there and stay while I do the workout?'

'I'd be pleased to. It would be wonderful to have you more mobile.

When do you want to go?'

'Today, if possible. I'll give them a call and see if there are any vacancies.'

'I'll just go and put some washing in and be back in a mo.'

'Oh goodness, I'd forgotten about that, Maria used to do it most days. The boys will have lots of dirty things.'

'They do. I'll collect them and is it OK if I do my own things at the same time?'

'Of course. I have a load or two of ours, as well. Goodness, without Maria, everything is falling apart.'

'I'll do my best. May not be quite up to Maria's standards but at least I'm not being a lazy girl.'

'Goodness me, you were never that. I'm just sorry to lumber you with all the things you're doing. At least Helga comes in today to clean round.'

'Thank goodness for that. I was wondering how I was going to fit that in.' Stella laughed.

When she came back up from the laundry, Isabel was on the phone, speaking in rapid Spanish.

'OK, Gracias. Gracias.' She switched off the phone and turned to Stella. 'They can see me this morning. Eleven o'clock. Hope that's OK with you.'

'Of course. Well done. I do hope it works and wouldn't it be wonderful if you really could walk again.'

'Amazing. Please, don't say anything to the family, will you? Especially not to Ignacio. I couldn't bear to give him hope and then let him down again. It could be helpful in the current circumstances if I really could try to walk again.'

'It will take a lot of persistence and patience and probably pain in the process. I know after trying to help my mum. It was different for her, I know.'

'Thank you so much for trying to help me. You are such a good friend.'

'Thank you. I'm pleased to be able to help in any way.'

'Let's have some coffee and then we can go.'

Under Arrest

It was a private health clinic and they arrived at what looked like a beautiful waiting room to Stella. She did give a thought as to how Isabel planned to pay but she seemed happy enough.

'May we speak in English for my friend?' Isabel asked.

'Of course, Señora. How are you getting on? It's quite a time since we saw you.' The immaculate receptionist spoke perfect English.

'As you can see, I'm almost totally wheelchair-bound. But I do feel my upper body strength is definitely improving. If only the legs would behave themselves, I'm sure I could walk again, using a walking frame of course. Oh sorry, this is my friend Stella. She's staying with us and is willing to help me.'

'How do you do.'

'Hello. How do you do.'

'Mr Davos will see you soon. He has a patient with him but his time is about up. Do take a seat.'

Five minutes later, Mr Davos came out of a side room and showed his client to the receptionist. He was a small Indian gentleman who almost bowed to the two women who were waiting.

'Come this way. Do you need help wheeling Senora Mendoza?' He spoke with a beautifully clear accent.

'No, thank you. I'm fine,' Stella answered.

They went into a room with various apparatus around the edge. A nurse was also in attendance, putting fresh paper on the bed and wiping surfaces. She nodded and greeted them.

'I assume you are here to see if you've improved? I have your notes here and see it's been almost a year since I saw you.'

'You're right. I'd so love to be able to walk again. I can almost stand by myself.'

'OK. Show me.' Isabel struggled hard and almost managed to stand on her wobbly legs. She was holding on to the wheelchair arms as she did so and she then collapsed back to her seat.

'I can almost manage it but not quite. Do you think there's something I can do?'

'We can try some exercises and if you try using the parallel bars, it might work. You're right. You do have good upper body strength. Let's try it and see if you can stand.'

Stella wheeled her over to the parallel bars and stood behind her.

'Use the bars to help you to stand. Use them to pull yourself up and out of the chair. Take your feet off the foot rests first.' Stella folded them out of the way.

'Right,' Isabel breathed, gritting her teeth and preparing to make for her, what seemed like a superhuman effort. She put her hands on the bars and took a deep breath and pulled herself up.

She wobbled but kept herself up

there, her hands shaking but clutching the wooden bars. She even managed a faint smile. Her hands grew less wobbly and she was standing for several seconds before she flopped back into the chair.

'Well done. I can see you are very determined. Don't expect too much too soon. Build on it gradually, allowing yourself to stand for more each time. Now, do you want to try it again?'

'All right,' Isabel replied. The second time she pulled herself up and stood for almost half a minute before she flopped back.

'Good. Before we go any further, I want you to exercise your legs. No use making yourself stand on limbs that are not strong enough.'

The rest of their session was spent doing leg strengthening exercises.

'Do you have someone who can help you to do this? It's important to manipulate your legs and with someone pushing them, it will make all the difference.'

'I can do it if you show me how,' Stella said.

'Well, you've seen how I was moving them. Come on, stand here and I will show you.'

Stella did as she was told and started to manipulate Isabel's legs. It felt strangely intimate and she felt apologetic.

'Don't worry. You are really going to help me,' Isabel told Stella.

After an hour, their appointment was over. They both felt exhausted, both physically and emotionally. They were fairly quiet on the drive back. Stella put a small lunch together for them both and they sat outside on the terrace to eat it.

'I think we'll do the usual pizza supper tonight. The boys will enjoy it and it makes everything seem more normal,' Isabel said.

'Sorry, but can we afford it?' Stella asked.

'It's not all that expensive. I'm sure it will be all right. Ignacio will want to go there. He always enjoys it. He did give me a bundle of notes yesterday so he obviously has money put on one side.'

Stella gave a shrug. At least it let her off doing the cooking.

'Don't forget, you mustn't mention our trip this morning. I don't want him to know anything about it. He might get his hopes unrealistically high.'

'Of course I won't say anything. I'm sorry again, but how are you going to pay for it? I mean it's all quite expensive, isn't it?'

'I do have private health care. It's my own policy so Ignacio won't ever see any reference to it. Don't worry, my dear, I do know what I'm doing.' She held her hand out to Stella and gave it a squeeze when she put her own hand out.

'Now, are you going to ask Stefano to join us this evening? Give him a call. Go on.'

'I don't like to interrupt them.' Isabel went out of the room and Stella hesitated but then she picked up the phone and called the number he'd given her.

'Sanchez,' came the voice.

'Stefano? It's Stella.'

'Oh, hello.'

'Is it a good time?'

'Not really. Is anything wrong?'

'Nothing. I just wanted to invite you to join us for pizzas this evening. The usual place.'

'Thank you. I must go now.' He hung up. Stella cursed herself for bothering him. It was obviously not a good time to have called.

She cleared away their lunch things and once more, loaded the dishwasher. She realised how boring housework was . . . much more than when she was at home and just had her mother to look after.

A family of five or six took much more thought. She switched the machine on and slumped down on a stool. What on earth was going to happen here? They couldn't go on like this indefinitely.

She was willing to help out during the current crisis but she wasn't much of a cook and in any case, this wasn't what she was here for. At least the house had been cleaned while they were out so she was spared from having to do that.

Then she remembered the washing she'd put in before they went out. She went down to the laundry and put it into the tumble dryer. Isabel had said she needed some washing doing so she went back upstairs wearily and knocked on Isabel's door.

'Did you want some washing doing?' she asked.

'I'm sorry but yes. There are shirts of Ignacio's and some undies and stuff of mine. Do you mind?'

'Course not,' she replied. She collected a full linen basket and took it down. There really was too much for one load but she stuffed it in, anyway.

She heard the phone ringing and assumed Isabel would answer it. When she got back upstairs, Isabel was looking very white and shocked.

'Ignacio has been arrested. They've taken him to the Guardia Civil HQ.'

'Oh, my goodness.' Stella hesitated. Dare she ask if Stefano was with him?

'Stefano has also been taken in for questioning.'

'No wonder he was hesitant when I spoke to him earlier. Whatever is going to happen? Do you know what he's been accused of?'

'Not really. He just said he was being arrested and taken in. I have no idea what is going to happen next.'

'Is there anything we can do?'

'I don't think so. He wasn't able to say much except they were going to the HQ. We just have to carry on as normal, I suppose. Collect the boys and well, I suppose we feed them at home.'

'I'm so sorry. Terrible thing to happen. Do you want to come with me to fetch the boys?'

'I don't know. Maybe. Perhaps not. Oh, I don't know. I can't think straight.'

'I know what you mean. Decide

soon, anyway. I need to leave in a quarter of an hour.'

Stella went to her room and sat down on her bed. She thought about Stefano and how he was with her. He had asked her if she thought they might have a future together but now, it looked as if he might be imprisoned, along with Ignacio.

How would the boys cope with it all? How would Isabel manage without her husband? However brave she was about learning to walk again, it would take many months and she would need considerable help in the meantime.

Stella thought she had better go and collect the two little boys and hoped to goodness they'd cope with the changes in their lives.

'Are you coming with me to fetch them?' she asked when she saw Isabel sitting staring out of the window.

'I might as well. If I stay here I'm only getting depressed. What a mess.'

The boys came out of school, bouncing with excitement. It was a

Friday after all and they loved Fridays. It was pizza night . . . only tonight, they were going to be disappointed.

'What time are we going out?' Juan asked.

'We're not tonight. Daddy's had to go away for a while and as there's only us, we're staying at home.'

'Oh, no. That's boring.'

'Tell you what,' Stella said, suddenly inspired. 'We have a build your own pizza night at home.'

'How does that work?' Javier demanded.

'I'll make a pizza base and you can choose what topping you want to put on yours. If we call at the supermarket, we can buy what we need. What do you think, Mummy?' Stella asked.

'That sounds like a splendid idea. Thank you.' She looked as if she might burst into tears. 'I haven't brought my purse with me, though.'

'It's all right. I have mine. Come on, then, boys, let's go and see what they've got in here. Are you coming in or staying in the car, Isabel?'

'I'll stay here, thanks.'

The two boys almost ran into the supermarket and both picked up a basket and started putting things in each.

'Hold on, you two. We don't need two lots of tomatoes or two lots of peppers. Put one of the baskets back and let's be scientific about how we're going to shop.

'Put one bag of tomatoes back and we shall only want one pepper. Let's move on to the cooked meat place.'

There were more arguments about whether they wanted ham or spicy slices of meat. In the end they took both so they could make their choices later.

'Cheese next,' she said. 'Then we need something to make the bases.'

'They sell bases over here,' Javier called out. 'Look, we can buy them to save making them.'

'Great,' Stella agreed. She wasn't sure how to actually make the bases so it was a bonus.

'Can we get them for Daddy and Stefano? They'll want them if they come back early.'

'I suppose so. They'll always keep for a while.'

The mention of their names hit her hard, making her think all over again about what was going to happen to them all. She realised she had been thinking they were both guilty and that also shocked her.

Suppose they were innocent and had been cheated out of the product they had been working on? Could they have been hacked? Whatever the reason, it all meant that Ignacio had lost a fortune and somehow, they would have to manage.

The two boys were hovering round a stand that sold chocolate. Stella relented and bought them a block each.

'For later,' she told them. 'After pizza time.'

Soon they were driving home again and once there, they went to change out of school clothes. Isabel was very grateful and told her how much she appreciated all Stella was doing for her and the children.

'That was quite inspired, your idea of build your own pizzas. Can you manage to make the bases?'

'No need. I got them ready made. It's just a case of loading them. The boys wanted me to buy one each for Ignacio and Stefano. I thought it was rather sweet.'

'I wonder if they will come home? Ignacio seemed very concerned. Hardly said anything on the phone. Seems a world away from this morning when I foolishly thought I was going to walk again. I'll forget about that now.'

'I don't think you should. If your private health care plan will pay for physio, then why not.'

'I'll have to pay the next instalment soon anyway and I won't have any spare money. No, I have to forget it. It would be much too long a process anyway.'

'But I can help you get fitter. Mr Davos showed me what to do. I can't let you slump back into that wheelchair without even trying.' Stella sounded quite fierce.

'Well, thank you. I will think about it.'

'No, you'll do it. I shall insist. I used to help my mother with movement so it won't be anything new to me. She used to protest and didn't want to do it whenever she felt tired. I kept her moving for at least an extra year.'

'Thank you for caring. It's very good of you, whatever happens.' She fell silent and once more looked a little teary.

'Goodness, I need to move some washing. I've left some in the tumble dryer for hours. Your stuff then needs to go in. I'll go and see to it now.'

The pizza-building session went very well. Stella produced a sort of tomato sauce to spread on the bases and then the boys took over. The pizzas were distinctly messy and far from professional-looking but the boys were delighted. She had a hot oven waiting and the pizzas all went in.

'We need to lay the table,' she instructed.

'Can't we eat in here?' Juan asked. 'It's more fun in here.'

'OK. Get out knives and forks and put them round. I'll get plates ready.'

'What are you and Mum going to have to drink?' Javier asked. 'Can we have fizzy pop?'

'If there is some. Where is it kept?'

'I'll get it. Do you want beer?'

'Well, it would be nice. If there is any. I didn't buy any more yesterday.'

'Dad keeps a supply in his office. I'll go and get some,' Juan offered. 'Can I go into his office?'

'Well, yes, as long as you don't touch anything.'

Juan trotted into the office and came out moments later looking rather shocked.

'It's a terrible mess in there. You should go and take a look.'

She did as he suggested and came away looking equally shocked.

'You're right, Juan. But there's nothing we can do to tidy it up. I'll bring the glasses out and wash them but as for all the papers everywhere, I don't think we should touch them.

'I'll go and get the dirty glasses and then perhaps we should lock the door. I'll ask Mummy if she has a key. Now, let's look at these pizzas. They should be done by now.'

They may not have been quite up to the restaurant's standards but they were delicious and they all enjoyed them. Even Isabel agreed they were good and she was delighted they had managed an evening without Ignacio's presence.

'Can we do this again next week?' Javier asked. 'I liked mine better than the restaurant ones. And can we have our chocolate now?'

'Chocolate as well?' Isabel feigned surprise.

'Yes.' Javier nodded vigorously. 'Stella bought us a block each.'

'That was very kind of her, wasn't it?

What on earth would we do without her?'

Juan stared at his mother.'

'Why do you say that? She isn't leaving, is she?'

'Of course not. We hope not, anyway.'

'You don't get rid of me that easily,' Stella told them. 'Eat your chocolate and then it's nearly bed time.'

'We can't go to bed before Daddy comes home. Not on a Friday. He's always home on Fridays.'

'I'm sorry but not tonight. I'm sure Stella will read you a story. I'll load the dishwasher and she can see you to bed and read a story.'

'You can't load the dishwasher. You know you can't,' Juan insisted. 'The last time you tried, you broke a lot of plates.'

'Well, perhaps I'm better at it doing it now.'

'Or you can leave it and I'll do it after I've put them to bed.'

'I shall try. If you hear a crash, you'll know I failed. At least eating in the kitchen means I don't have far to go. Goodnight now, you two imps.'

'We're not imps. We're boys,' Javier protested.

'OK. Goodnight then, boys. Give Mummy a kiss.'

It was almost an hour later before Stella sank down in her favourite armchair. Isabel handed her a drink, having carefully wheeled across the room.

'See? I'm getting more independent. Ignacio usually insists on doing that sort of thing. I wonder where he is now.' She gave a long sigh. 'Perhaps I ought to have taken some of his things in to him.'

'You probably wouldn't be allowed to see him.'

'If he isn't home tomorrow, I shall insist on seeing him.'

'I wonder if Stefano's family know where he is? Do you think I should telephone them?'

'I'm not sure. I'd think he would have used his call to telephone them.

He might even be at home already.'

'I think he'd have called me if that was the case. Maybe he would. Or perhaps he wouldn't as Ignacio is still being held. Oh, what a mess it all is. I hate this not knowing what's happening.'

It reached eleven o'clock and they had heard nothing. The two women decided to go to bed and see what the next day brought. Stella lay in her bed and suddenly remembered the washing. It was still in the tumble drier. It would be creased beyond recognition if it was left there any longer.

She pulled on a dressing gown and pattered downstairs to rescue it. She pulled it out and put it into a washing basket. She heard a sudden noise coming from the garage. With great trepidation she pushed open the laundry door and peered round. Ignacio's car drove in and the doors were closed.

'Ignacio? Is that you?' she called softly.

'Yes. What are you doing?'

'Nothing really. Sorting some washing I'd forgotten.'

'But it's nearly midnight. I'd hoped to sneak in quietly and sleep somewhere and be here in the morning.'

'Isabel would never forgive you. What's been happening?'

'I've been bailed. I'm still charged, unfortunately. Me and Stefano. There will be a trial fairly soon but in the meantime, I'm under restrictions. A sort of house arrest. Stefano has the same thing applied to him.'

'Can I go and see him?'

'I suppose so. But now, if I don't find somewhere to sleep, I shall fall down. I will go to Isabel if you think she'll welcome me.'

'Of course she will. Goodnight.'

'Goodnight. And leave that darned washing, please.'

Stella shrugged and followed him upstairs. She went on up to her room and peeped in at the boys. They were both sound asleep. She went into her own room and flopped down on the bed. What a day it had been.

From this morning when she had taken Isabel to the physio clinic to sorting washing late this evening, she had scarcely stopped all day.

And with all the worry added to it, it seemed to have gone on for ever. Stella closed her eyes and almost instantly fell asleep.

When she awoke the next morning, she almost wondered if she had been dreaming and Ignacio had never come home. Then she heard a delighted yell from the boys.

'Daddy, Daddy, you came back!'

'We had a build your own pizza supper. It was magic. Much better than the restaurant.'

Stella smiled. At least something she had organised had gone well.

She Loves Me!

The following days were rather stressful. Ignacio did not take well to being stuck at home and he walked back and forth across the lounge, muttering to himself.

He didn't even have a computer he could use as they had been impounded. The Guardia Civil had also taken the boys' computer and Ignacio's telephone. They had wanted to cut off the house landline but Isabel had complained about that, concerned she might need medical help at some time.

Stella was still driving the boys to school and she did call on Stefano at his home. She felt it was all rather difficult and he eventually asked her not to call again until he was released from his ban. Stella wasn't happy about that but felt she had no option but to agree.

'But what about shopping? Won't

your mother need shopping?'

'We have neighbours who are willing to help,' Stefano said. 'But thank you for your thought.'

'Well, please ask me if there's anything you need. I'm doing our shopping most days so it isn't a problem.'

'Thank you. I'd better go now and see about making some lunch.'

Stella drove away, thinking she might not see him again. But she tried to tell herself she was being overly dramatic and tried to smile.

She stopped at the supermarket and pulled out her purse. Ignacio had given her some more notes so she didn't have to rely on using her card. She soon filled her trolley and paid for everything. She couldn't help wondering where the cash was coming from but it was nothing to do with her and she had to accept it.

What had happened to the gentle au pair job she had applied for? She now seemed to be the mainstay of the whole household, cooking, washing and still looking after the boys. Her days were long and very busy.

She wasn't sure how much longer she could go on for but there was no way she could ever say anything either to Ignacio or Isabel.

In all honesty, Ignacio could have done a whole lot more to help but it wasn't her place to say anything. Besides, he was under immense stress, she conceded.

Conversations seemed to revolve around Isabel suggesting they leave their home and sell it and Ignacio saying the Guardia Civil should get their act together and find out the real perpetrators of the crimes they had endured.

'Perhaps I should apply for some sort of aid,' Isabel suggested. 'Many people in my situation get financial help from the government. We really need to get a cook. It's not fair for Stella to have to do it every day and I can't manage more than peeling a few vegetables.'

'I suppose you think I should be doing it,' Ignacio snapped. His attitude was so out of character to the lovely man Stella had first met. Stella listened carefully to Isabel's reply.

'There are some things you could do. Tidy your study for one thing. There are papers everywhere. Why not spend this time sorting that lot out?'

He said nothing and went to the door and tried it.

'It seems to be locked. I can't get into it. Was that the police, too?'

'No, I did it to keep the boys out. Once I saw the mess I decided I'd lock it. The key is in the bedroom.'

Silently, he went to the bedroom and came back with the key. He went inside his study and slammed the door shut.

Isabel turned to Stella.

'I'm sorry. You shouldn't have to hear us arguing.'

'No worries. I'll sort out something for lunch. I bought a frittata this morning. Will that do? With some salad.'

'That sounds great. Thank you so much for all you're doing. I know it's way beyond what you were expecting.'

'It's OK for now. I'm not sure how much longer I can go on doing it. As I said, I'm not much of a cook. You must be sick of some of my efforts and long to go back to your special Spanish delights.'

'Oh, my dear, not at all. The boys are enjoying some good English food. Everything you've done so far has been excellent. But we can't go on like this. I don't know how much more money Ignacio has got stashed away in there. He won't even tell me where it came from but that's the least of my worries.'

There was a sudden crash from the study followed by a loud shout.

'What's wrong?' Isabel asked, shouting towards the door. Ignacio came out waving a folder and almost shouting with delight.

'I've just realised who has put us into this situation. This folder makes it obvious and it's all so clear.'

'Who or what? Tell me quickly.'

'There was a salesman belonging to one of our rivals. He spent time in my office one day when he was waiting for me. I didn't realise he was there and one of my stupid girls let him sit in there for possibly half an hour.

'Then he left without seeing me. I've just found a document that came from his company which condemns him somewhat. I'd forgotten all about him. He must have had enough time to download the material he wanted from my computer and managed to sit on the other side of my desk looking all innocent.

'I must phone the police right away. They must believe me.'

'Oh, Ignacio. I do hope so. Phone them now, right away.'

Stella was listening in the background, having come into the room at his shout. She crossed to Isabel and took her hand.

'Fingers crossed,' she whispered.

'Couldn't help hearing. That's wonderful news, assuming they believe him of course. It must mean Stefano is also in the clear. But who could have been stupid enough to leave anyone in his office?'

'I'm not sure what Ignacio's found but it was something in his office. It was such a mess in there, I'm not surprised it had fallen out of the process. He's on the phone now.'

All Stella could hear was a burble of Spanish with Ignacio sounding rather urgent and also rather cross. Obviously he wasn't making his point strongly enough. She waited patiently for him to finish to see what was going to happen.

At last he put the phone down and came out of his office looking somewhat angry. He also looked decidedly sheepish. The two women looked at each other and back at him, waiting for him to explain.

'I didn't know it but that wretched girl was working in the office.'

'Which wretched girl?'

'I really didn't recognise her. I would never have employed her. Her skills are useless . . . well, whatever skills she is supposed to have.'

'But who?' Isabel asked in frustration. 'Who are you talking about.'

'Maria's niece! The one you turned down for a job here. Evidently she was employed on a temporary basis by one of the other people. I never saw her.

'She left the salesman in my office and even showed him where I kept private things. She'd found that out when I was away one day. Honestly.' He cursed in Spanish and Stella was quite glad she didn't understand him.

'Stupid people. They simply don't get the message at all. They need to contact the firm I gave them and question this salesman who wasn't a salesman at all, of course. I reckon he was sent to our company to get this information. He was someone Maria and her niece knew. They knew we had something important in the pipeline and voila, they got it.

'How can I convince them? I'm still not supposed to leave the house and they need to see this paper. It makes everything clear.'

'I could take it to the HQ if that's any help,' Stella offered. 'There must be someone there who speaks English.'

'Oh, there is. It's Diego Martin you'd need to see. OK, this may be the answer. Make sure you give it directly to him. Don't give it to anyone else. Do you understand?'

'Of course,. But I have to collect the boys in about an hour or less. Will I have time to go the HQ before then? I'm not even sure where it is.'

'I could go with her to guide her,' Isabel offered.

'Go then. Go. Go. You'll just make it in time.'

Isabel went down in the lift and Stella ran down the stairs. The wheel-chair was still in the back of the boot so she left the electric wheelchair near the car and got in. Her instructions were quite clear and it didn't take very long for them to reach the HQ.

'You go in. Diego Martin is dealing with the case,' she reminded Stella.

'Yes, I've got that.' She went into the HQ and saw the officer on the desk. 'Do you speak English?' she asked.

'Leetle bit. What you want?'

'I need to see Diego Martin. It's very urgent.'

'He busy man.'

'Yes but I need to give him this.' She indicated the folder.

'I take it.'

'No, I have to give it to him.'

'He busy man. Much too busy for you.'

'It's to do with Ignacio Mendoza.'

'He too busy.'

'Oh, please. Give him a call.' She pointed at the phone.

'Can no do that.'

'I'll go and get Senora Mendoza to come in.'

'Who is that?'

'Never mind.' She rushed out and asked Isabel if she would come in. 'I can't get through to the officer on the desk. He says Diego is too busy.'

'Get my chair out of the back. I'll certainly come in and sort him out.'

Stella fetched her chair round to the door and she eased herself into it. She went inside and in her own fluent Spanish told the man it was vital she saw Diego Martin.

Stella could see her being told he was a busy man and smiled as she told him she would have his job taken off him if he didn't fetch him right away. At least, that's what Stella assumed she was saying.

The officer disappeared and came back a few moments later followed by a smart-looking, if irritable, man.

Again, Isabel spoke in Spanish and wanted him to see the document in the folder. She flicked her fingers at Stella who stepped forward with it. He promised to read it soon, Isabel told her.

'Come on, the boys will be waiting for us.'

Stella drove as quickly as was safe and found the two boys waiting in the classroom with one of the teachers. Javier was in tears and Juan was trying to comfort him. When they saw Stella, they ran to her happily.

'I thought you'd gone away and left us,' Javier sobbed.

'I'm so sorry,' Stella said. 'Your daddy wanted me to take a letter to the Guardia Civil. It took me a while to find the right person. Your mum's in the car. Come on, let's not keep her waiting.'

Ignacio was anxiously waiting for their return and Isabel told him what happened.

'I think it may take him some time to read it. But at least you are here at home and as long as you don't go out, it won't be too bad for you.'

'I can't tell you how I'm looking forward to going out. I want to take us all out for a beautiful meal and spend the evening relaxing.'

'Soon, my love. Soon.'

It took another week before they came to tell Ignacio he was completely in the clear. They had arrested several people at the rival business and the information was restored to Ignacio's company. Stefano was also cleared and he rushed round to see Stella. He took her out into the garden.

'I can't tell you how much I was longing to see you. I told you not to come in case I was to be imprisoned. I didn't want you waiting for me outside and be unable to see you. I love you, Stella. Please say you care just a little bit for me.'

'Of course I do. I never realised it till I could no longer see you. I was so miserable but now, everything's going to be fine.'

'So you care for me only a little bit.'

'No. I care a lot. In fact, I love you.'

'And will you marry me?'

'I should think so.'

'Let's go and tell everyone. I could

shout it from the roof tops. She loves me! We're going to be married!'

She told him to stop shouting it but he took no notice. He grabbed her hand and dragged her into the house.

'Guess what? Stella loves me and has agreed to be my wife. What do you think of that?'

'But who will do our cooking and fetch us from school?' Javier asked.

'We'll have to find another cook and maybe another au pair.'

'But we don't want another au pair. We like Stella.'

'We all like Stella.'

'I can still fetch you from school each day and probably take you to school, too. Nothing will change for a bit, anyway. Weddings take a while to plan.'

'Not ours. It will happen very quickly, I'm determined — before she gets a chance to change her mind.' Stefano was laughing as he spoke but Isabel intervened.

'Oh, no, you don't. Stella must have a proper wedding.

'It will take ages to get her dress and there are the flowers to organise and the wedding feast. We can't have any old things.'

'We could have a build your own pizza evening instead of a feast,' Juan suggested with enthusiasm.

'Everyone would like that, you know they would.'

They all laughed.

'Sounds like a plan,' Stella agreed.

WHERE THE HEART IS
OUT OF THE BLUE
TOMORROW'S DREAMS
DARE TO LOVE
WHERE LOVE BELONGS
TO LOVE AGAIN
DESTINY CALLING
THE SURGEON'S MISTAKE
GETTING A LIFE
ONWARD AND UPWARD
THE DAIRY
TIME FOR CHANGE
BROKEN PROMISES
THE PLOT THICKENS
MEETING MOLLY